I0631198

R. S. Dement

Ingersoll, Beecher and Dogma

R. S. Dement

Ingersoll, Beecher and Dogma

ISBN/EAN: 9783337145026

Printed in Europe, USA, Canada, Australia, Japan

Cover: Foto ©Andreas Hilbeck / pixelio.de

More available books at **www.hansebooks.com**

INGERSOLL, BEECHER

AND

DOGMA,

OR

A FEW SIMPLE TRUTHS

AND THEIR LOGICAL DEDUCTIONS,

IN WHICH THE POSITIONS OF

MR. INGERSOLL AND MR. BEECHER

ARE CONSIDERED IN TWO LECTURES.

ENTITLED

MEPHISTO-MINOTAURUS

AND

THE ABSOLUTE NECESSITIES.

R. S. DE___NT.

CHI___

S. C. GRIGGS ___

18___

AUTHOR'S PREFATORY REMARKS.

THE wonders of the kaleidoscope are but the reflec-
tions of numerous pieces of colored glass, rough, without
symmetry, unsightly in themselves, having no connection
with each other, and but very trifling value. If we take
these little pieces out of the case that is artfully arranged
for them, and examine them, each upon its own individual merits, or collectively as a whole, we shall be surprised
that any art could have succeeded in causing us to think
them of beauty or of value. The author well remem-
bers the feeling when, a child, he solved the mystery of
his first kaleidoscope. He felt that he had been imposed
upon—deceived into believing that what he saw was at
least the shadow of something real and beautiful, when in
truth it was only a delusion ; and he has been skeptical of
appearances ever since. And so, when Mr. Ingersoll put
his bits of painted words, bits of highly-colored thoughts,
and bits of Infidel philosophy, and a great variety of
nondescript bits and broken fragments of all kinds, into
his kaleidoscopic lecture of " The Gods," and placed it
on sale in almost all the shops of the land, the author se-
cured a copy, and true to his early lesson, set about solving its mysteries. In the lecture, " Mephisto-Minotaurus,"
will be found the result of his investigation.

What Mr. Ingersoll has put together in the work referred
to is, no doubt, to many minds, of very questionable value,
unless some of it be classed with the antiquities, and with

this part the market is already glutted ; but when he puts it between the polished glasses of his wit, his satire and his eloquence, and whirls it round with magic swiftness, there is to one's eyes, bewildered by his art, a wonderful and entrancing vision.

In reviewing Mr. Beecher's philosophy, the author has not confined himself so exclusively to the text. He has sought rather to consider what appeared to him the irreconcilable dogmas of many of our religious societies, and in the treatment of this subject he has sought to be governed solely by the merits of *the ideas themselves*, without attaching any importance to the *sources* from which they may have emanated. In the lecture entitled "The Absolute Necessities," will be found the offering he brings to the altar of thought, trusting that at least some incense will arise from it to join the "pillar of cloud by day and the pillar of fire by night," which shall lead us on in the march of soul to the Infinite.

The author expressly desires to be understood that in the title of his work he intends no disrespect to either of the illustrious names with which he adorns it, and trusts that neither Mr. Ingersoll nor Mr. Beecher will feel compromised by being associated together.

R. S. DEMENT.

CHICAGO, March, 1878.

MEPHISTO-MINOTAURUS.

The conflict of faith and unbelief remains the proper, the only, the deepest theme of the history of the world and mankind, to which all others are subordinate.

GOETHE.

With the vulgar and the learned, Names have great weight; the wise use a writ of inquiry into their legitimacy when they are advanced as authorities.

ZIMMERMAN.

For 'tis the sport to have the engineer
Hoist with his own petar.

SHAKSPEARE.

MEPHISTO-MINOTAURUS.*

EVERY age has produced remarkable men.
Occasional ages have shown us men who were
truly great. It has seldom been the case, however, that a man was correctly measured by
the age in which he lived. Indeed, it has not
always been the case that men have been
rightly judged by *subsequent* ages. And how
seldom have been the instances where the
career of a man has been *foretold* to any degree of accuracy ! And how very seldom that
a master has succeeded to that prophetic art
which has produced an accurate portrait of a
man who was yet to be born ! Indeed I know
of but one such instance. It stands out in re-

* It is not intended to reflect upon Mr. Ingersoll personally in
anything that is offered in these pages. It is only so far as he is
identified with his theories, by his manner of putting them, that
we allude to him, here, as a sort of personation of his philosophy.

lief, solitary and alone. I desire to speak of
it. It is, really, quite remarkable.

The portrait to which I refer may be found
in an essay, written half a century ago, by an
eminent and distinguished author. I will show
it you, only reserving the name of the hero.
The likeness will at once be recognized. Here
it is:

"Our hero is a cultivated personage, and
acquainted with the modern sciences; sneers
at witchcraft and the black art, even while em-
ploying them as heartily as any member of the
French Institute; for he is a *philosophe*, and
doubts most things, nay, half disbelieves even
his own existence.

"It is not without cunning effort that all this
is managed; but managed in a considerable
degree, it is; for a world is opened to us which,
we might almost say, we feel to be at once true
and not true. . . . Doubtless our hero has
the manners of a gentleman; he knows the
world; nothing can exceed the easy tact with
which he manages himself; his wit and sar-
casm are unlimited; the cool, heartfelt con-

tempt with which he despises all things, human
and divine, might make the fortune of half a
dozen fellows about town. . . . He is sometimes called the *Denier*, and this truly is his
name; for as Voltaire did with historical doubt,
so does he with all moral appearances—settles
them with a *N'en croyez rien.*

"The shrewd, all-informed intellect he has,
is an attorney intellect; it can contradict but
it cannot affirm. With lynx vision he descries
at a glance the ridiculous, the unsuitable, the
bad; but for the solemn, the noble, the worthy,
he is blind.

"Thus does he go along, qualifying, confut-
ing, despising; on all hands detecting the false,
but without force to bring forth, or even to
discern, any glimpse of the true.

"Poor fellow; what truth should there be
for him? To see falsehood is his only truth;
falsehood and evil are the rule; truth and
good, the exception which confirms it. He
can believe in nothing but his own self-conceit
and in the indestructible baseness, folly, and
hypocrisy of men. . . . At humanity he

has no grudge ; he merely operates by way of
experiment, to pass the time scientifically.

" Such a combination of logical Life and
moral Death, so universal a *Denier*, both in
heart and head, is undoubtedly a child of Dark-
ness, an emissary of the Primeval Nothing ;
and coming forward, as he does, like a person
of breeding, and without any flavor of brim-
stone, may stand here, in his merely spiritual
deformity, at once potent, dangerous and con·
temptible."

This is an extract from an essay by Thomas
Carlyle, contributed to the *Foreign Review*, in
1828. It had, at the time, a world·wide fame
as a pen-portrait of Mephistopheles. Indeed,
Mr. Carlyle humored this interpretation him·
self ; it served as a mask for his hero. A mad
rogue for a jest was Carlyle in those days, and
how cleverly did he play this one on his critics
and reviewers ; and how capitally did he con·
ceal his design ! How he must have chuckled
and laughed to himself as he realized that in
less than half a century the true hero of his
portraiture should be recognized ! When his

"picture of Mephistopheles" should be regarded in its true light as a prophetic vision
of Ingersollism.

This much as an *introduction*, merely, to the
first half of our heading — the Mephisto.

A word or two only will be necessary as an
introduction to the second part — the Mino-
taurus. It will be found eminently fitting
when brought in direct application to the
hero of this paper.

Now, the Minotaur of the Grecians was the
result of a *liaison*, the history of which is familiar to readers. Our Ingersoll is the result
of a *liaison* between what he is, himself, pleased
to name, respectively, " Reason " and " Philosophy."

[It may be as well, right here, to borrow a
brace of Dr. Holmes' brackets, and drop in an
item in reference to a peculiarity of our hero
as contradistinguished from his fellow Ameri-
cans, and from those with whom he has sought
fellowship, his cousins-german.

The distinction is a marked one, for while
with the former, titles such as " Hon." etc.,

and with the latter, those of " Von," etc., are
seldom if ever omitted, our Ingersoll, invariably, when mentioning the names of his illustrious parentage referred to (Reason and Philosophy), omits a prefix which belongs to both
alike, and applies directly to both with as positive significance.   I refer to the little Greek
word *Pseudo.*

Since Mr. Ingersoll has omitted to mention
so important an ear-mark of his progenitors,
and in order that we may not become confused
in tracing the descent of species, it will, perhaps, be well to take a cue from Mr. Darwin,
and compound a word to suit the emergency ;
and since our hero presumes to the *ermine*
of his class, what more appropriate title than
His Pseudolency?   This will avoid the necessity of frequent references to his great origi-
nals, False Reason and False Philosophy.]

With this understanding we will proceed.
Now, the analogy before us becomes all the
more striking when we realize that the result
of the *liaison* in the one instance was the production of as great a monstrosity as in the

other, for His Pseudolency is, surely, as Mino-
taurian a specimen of humanity as our ancient
Grecian brethren, with all the wealth of their
fertile imaginations, could have possibly conceived of. Unlike the iconoclasts of a more
refined order, he disdains the hammer of argument, but plunges in among the idols of
antiquity, and, with a bellowing and roaring
that all but shakes the foundations of Olympus, more than an ocean's breadth away, gores
and smashes things indiscriminately.

In more direct reference to our analogue
we will now proceed to consider his works,
with a touch at the life and character of our
hero, wherein the further aptitude of our
nomen omen will, no doubt, appear.

Of course Mr. Ingersoll, the citizen, and
Mr. Ingersoll, the philosopher, are two very
different persons. We make no allusion to
citizen Ingersoll. He may be a very esti-
mable friend and gentleman for aught I
know. It is with Mr. Ingersoll, the Pseudo-
philosopher, that we have to do.

We will open his book.

" THE GODS

"A N D   O T H E R   L E C T U R E S ,

" BY

" ROBERT G. INGERSOLL.

" Give me the storm and tempest of thought
" and action, rather than the dead calm
, " of ignorance and faith. Banish me
" from Eden when you will ; but
" first let me eat of the
" tree of Knowledge.
" PEORIA, ILLINOIS :
" 1874."

Let us begin with the very title-page. To
the first of the two sentences with which this
page is ornamented, I have simply to say:
Bravo ! Give *me* the storm and tempest of
thought and action, rather than the dead
calm of ignorance and faith.

But in passing to the second, one is convulsed
with laughter ! The idea of His Pseudolency,
Mephisto-Minotaurus, running about loose in
Eden, refusing to be put out until he shall
first be permitted to breakfast from the tree

of Knowledge, is too much for one's midriff. The figure employed would not be quite so bad were it not for His Pseudolency's dual character. Now, were he simply Mephisto, he might set up a sort of claim to a temporary lien on the aforesaid garden, by virtue of a former title of occupancy vested in an early and somewhat illustrious member of the Mephistophelian family. But it is highly probable that his Snakeship has already taken the double nature of his immediate heir into account and made other provision for him—possibly, somewhere near Tartarus, down below Avernus, and so even the shadow of title referred to fades from our vision. But to think of his roaring and bellowing and pawing through that beautiful garden, throwing up a great cloud of dust to blind us from his true purpose, is altogether too funny to be endurable.

Turning a leaf, we find the "preface," which we discover to be an illustrated one; and perhaps there never was a preface that so completely represented what was to follow it as

this. It is at the same time a sort of frontis-
piece, representing at the top of the page three
crosses, on two of which are suspended human
forms as in crucifixion, and at the foot of the
third cross, which stands between the other
two, are a number of women and children being
burned as heretics. Beneath this remarkable
conception are the words:

"For the Love of God."

At the bottom of the page there is a representation of three telegraph poles, resembling
somewhat the three crosses, with wires
stretched from each to each, and at the
bottom of this picture are the words:

"For the Use of Man."

Now, in justice to His Pseudolency, the
author of this remarkable cartoon (I take
for granted that the author of the book is the
author of its preface in this instance), it
should be stated that he is not really so stupid,
— for he is a man of rare genius and acknowledged ability — as to put an estimate upon it
above the most transparent and inconceivably
ridiculous clap-trap. He appreciates that it

is no more than this, quite as well as you or I. We must not lose sight of what Mr. Carlyle said of him before he was born, in the essay we have quoted: "At humanity he has no grudge; he merely operates by way of experiment, to pass the time scientifically."

No doubt, were he to express himself frankly in regard to this cartoon, he would admit, for he is very candid at times, that cartoons, as a rule, are low, very low, in fact. That should such a master as Nast undertake a job upon him and the disciples of " Reason " he could cartoon them beyond all endurance.

Take the history of Infidelity in France, for instance, where they ran so wild after " Reason " and " Liberty " that they positively paraded a common courtesan at the head of one of their grandest processions, and hailed her as the " Goddess of Reason."

Or right here in the United States of America, where thousands pin their souls to Mr. Ingersoll's coat-tails,— just imagine a whole herd of souls tied on as Nast could tie them

1*

as a sort of caudal appendage to His Pseudolency, Mephisto-Minotaurus!

And Mr. Ingersoll appreciates as well as
anybody else that the only possible *point* in
the picture, that might otherwise indirectly
seem to favor his side of the question, is lost
in the fact that the telegraph is pre-eminently
a Christian institution, and is indebted to
Christianity and to Christian enlightenment
for every stage of its continually advancing
improvement.

He ought to be capable of appreciating
another fact: that neither the genius nor the
spirit of Christianity is responsible for the
crimes that have been perpetrated under the
banner of the Cross.

Still less is it an argument against Christianity that wicked men have stolen her liv-
ery to cloak their infamy, or that misguided
zealots, in her name, have done such deeds as
have all earth and heaven turned thought-sick
and all hell amazed.

Why did not Mr. Ingersoll append to his
picture the representation of a steamboat,

railroad, telescope, spectroscope, telephone, church, college, or indeed any of the advance couriers of Christian enlightenment, and claim them for Infidelity, as well as the telegraph ? O, plumed knight of the brazen cheek ! verily thou hast almost compromised thyself right in the beginning !

We come now to the first of the remarkable lectures of this remarkable book.

THE GODS.

"*An honest God is the noblest work of man.*"

By the little line in italics, "*An honest God is the noblest work of man,*" it is presumed that His Pseudolency simply intended a little witticism, or pun, as it were — merely experimenting, you know — for the intensity of thought, the tension of nerve and brain, the heavy labor, so to speak, of His Pseudolency, that is evident throughout the lecture that follows to prove that the most damnable and ridiculous of *all* work that humanity can engage in is that of making gods, precludes the possibility that he could have attached any *meaning* to the little line in italics.

Following this is the lecture proper — and of all the anomalies of English literature it is surely the most remarkable! Walt Whitman's "Leaves of Grass" is nowhere in comparison.

Where to commence or how to commence a review is puzzling. If there were any defined line of argument — any firstlys, secondlys and thirdlys, the mile-posts of the old school — any landmarks, so to speak, of any kind — but so far from there being any defined *line* of argument, there is no *argument* at all. His Pseudolency has no argument to make ; he is simply a *Denier*, without argument ; this is the Mephisto part of him.

His pace cannot be measured, for he has neither regular gait, nor does he move in any prescribed direction—he simply plunges, now forward, now backward, now to either side — pawing and bellowing and raising a wonderful dust all the while ; this is the Minotaur part of him.

The only practical way that I can discern is to follow wherever there is a dust.

Mr. Ingersoll opens his lecture by stating that " Each nation has created a God."

This, I take it, was intended as a sort of poetic expression intended to convey the idea that all nations have had some sort of natural, instinctive or intuitional conception of an authority or power beyond their own — an overruling Deity. It either means this or it means nothing, and in the light of this interpretation I most heartily indorse it.

Mr. Ingersoll might, however, have been less obscure and more forcible by carrying the thought into all the existencies of the universe.

He could have begun with the vegetable world wherein he would have found :

First, Everything dependent upon a su-perior power.

Second, All things acting as if, seemingly, *conscious* of that superior power.

He would have found the First evinced in every state of development. He would have found the Second evinced in the *progress* of that development.

To be plainer : Had he gone to the ivy that

decks the tree in the forest, he had found
its delicate tendrils reaching out for help and
support to the bark and the twigs of its powerful friend; had he tried to unclasp its tiny
arms, he had found them clinging to their
stately protector with the tenacity of life itself.
Then had he stooped to the fern or the flower
at his feet, he had found them as seemingly
conscious of their dependence upon the Earth,
and resisting with all their puny strength his
efforts to tear them from her bosom. Then,
could he have listened to the voices of these,
the soft wave of sound that attends the unfold-
ing of the tiniest germ, he had heard a sweet
song, as of thankfulness, a song that rises up
from each infinitesimal stage of life, in the progress of its development. And he had found
all these, the stately oak, the tendriled ivy,
the delicate fern, and the fragrant flower, all
reaching their arms to the sun—the Divinity
of matter.

Then had he gone to the orders of animal life, he had found the same fact of dependence. He had found every living thing,

from the dawn of its being on to the end of its latest breath, imbued with the instinct or intuition of a Superior Power — a power beyond itself. The young that looks to the mother, the mother that looks to the sire, the sire that looks to its nobler brother in the species above it, and this brother to one still above it, on till the highest and noblest of animals that stands in awe of the child ; and the child looks up to the humblest man, and this man to the man who is great, and he to the Divinity of men.

And then, had he lifted his face to the stars, he might have learned that those innumerable systems of worlds revolve round their central suns, and that all these are dependent on law. And in these he would have found a design, and the design dependent upon a designer, and that that designer was the Divinity of worlds.

And then, had he opened the book of *thought*, he could have found a volume of *Unities*, and this would have taught him that the divinity of matter, and the divinity of

men, and the divinity of worlds, were *one*—
the trinity of perfection ; He whom the Christians call God.

And then he would, no doubt, have made
his opening sentence more accurate, by saying:
" Each nation has created an image of God."
And then, instead of his second sentence reading as it does : "And the god has always re-
sembled his creators," he would have made it
read as follows : " And that image of God has
conformed to the conceptions of its creators."
I say he *would* have done this ; of course this
is upon the hypothesis that he is an honest
man ; I accord to all men *honesty.*

Had he then have permitted a commendable
zeal for the truth, he would have added : " This
fact of dependence which we find throughout
the material world, and this *instinct of a superior power* which we find throughout all
orders of animals, and this *intuition of a God*
which we find throughout all conditions of humanity and all the ages of the world, — these
three absolute truths are a very conclusive
argument that there *is* One on whom all things

depend, a power beyond all animal life, a God who touches every soul through this intuitional link of Himself."

After the two sentences we have given, the first twelve pages appear to be devoted to an irregular dissertation on the gods of history. It is here that the Minotaur part takes entire control. He roars and bellows, and charges in among the idols of the past with all the fury of the most illustrious sires of his species. And yet he is altogether harmless, in these paroxysms, save to himself. The objects of his rage being simply myths, he charges through these in a cloud of dust — to his own exhaustion. Meeting no opposition save here and there from the rocks of truth that lie in his way, over these he but stumbles and falls to rise again in redoubled fury, foaming and roaring and lashing his sides for another attack. And so he returns again and again to his fight with the gods. He is safer, it would appear, from personal harm than was poor old Don Quixote, in his attack upon the windmills ; and yet it may be but for a time, for,

2

we are told, "though the mills of the gods grind slowly, yet they grind exceeding small," and if they do nothing else, they may still keep their spectral shadows dancing before His Pseudolency on the heights of Olympus till he shall butt his brains out at its base.

But in the name of reason, philosophy, common sense and uncommon sense, what has all this tirade of abuse, heaped upon the myths of the benighted ages of the past, to do with the negations of the Infidels of to-day? Wherein does all this historical slush and cheap wit affect the philosophy of the Christian religion? What relation has Christianity to Pagan idolatry? I thought that it was to *cure* all these ills, *heal* all these wounds, and lift humanity to a higher, nobler being, that the Christian philosophy was instituted. Suppose that all you have charged to the gods of antiquity be admitted — then what? Stuff and nonsense! Do you think your readers are a lot of idiots?

After this, my dear sir, do not address us as though we were so many consummate fools, or the sting of our self-respect will be apt to beget prejudice.

I trust my readers will pardon me for thus stepping aside occasionally to address His Pseudolency in person.

With the last half of page twelve (12) our author begins his comments upon the inhuman wars of the Old Testament.

" We are asked to justify these frightful passages, these infamous laws of war, because the bible is the word of God," says this apostle of reason. You are asked to do no such thing. You never were asked, and you never will be asked, to do any such thing by anybody with as much intelligence as it takes to put a proposition into simple English.

What you *are* asked is to take into consideration the stages of development through which the human race has passed since the wars of the Old Testament to reach what it now is, and then to recognize in the tribes of barbarians of those days the " people " against whom the "armies of invasion" were moving.

It would be a terrible chapter to read, two

thousand years from now, that the United States forces had cut down Sitting Bull and his people, and yet it may be doubted if even the god of reason would paralyze the uplifted arm of the government — if Mr. Sitting Bull could only be gotten hold of.

I am free to admit that there is much in the Old Testament history which, looked at from our distant perspective, is horrible and revolting; but we must not forget that *much of the Old Testament is simple history, setting up no claim to divine inspiration, except as to a faithful narration of facts*, events with which God had nothing to do, or for which he was no more responsible than He is for the present war in the East.

Were the history of the present Russo-Turkish war to be read two thousand years from now, it would, no doubt, stand recorded as a Christian war on the part of Russia, and the historian could offer abundant evidence for his statement, false as it would be.

So, no doubt, is much of the Old Testament history. There are many rulers who claim the authority of God who are really directed by the devil.

Because the United States is a Christian nation it does not follow that every ruler of the United States is a Christian, nor that if he gets into a drunken brawl or wages an unholy war that his acts are sanctioned by the Christians' God.

And, aside from all this, does Mr. Ingersoll find anything in the teachings of Christ that countenances war, or violence of any kind? Does he not *know* that the old law, that was made for the barbarous ages of the past, is *repealed* in the new?

How a *lawyer* of his excellent sagacity, not to speak of honesty, could make such a plea as he makes here is, certainly, very remarkable. But a personal acquaintance with Mr. Ingersoll makes his feigned horror of war extremely astonishing — to put it mildly.

To return to the text : " The instant that we admit that a book is too sacred to be reasoned about, we are mental serfs," says this politico-philosophe. Well, who disputes it?

Again : "It is infinitely absurd to suppose that a god would address a communication to intelligent beings, and yet make it a crime to be punished in eternal flames for them to use their intelligence for the purpose of understanding his communication." Who disputes it? Who ever heard of a god of that kind? O, Prince of Pettifoggers!

These are only samples of the sentences with which he crams his book. His favorite method seems to be to make a statement that nobody disputes, and then proceed to argue as though everybody that is not an Infidel *does* dispute it.

Here is a brace of them that he has standing out by themselves, as a sort of couplet — a pair of metaphysical twins, as it were :

"Salvation though slavery is worthless. Salvation from slavery is inestimable."

A question might arise, just here, as to whether His Pseudolency is a less slave to the teachings of Voltaire, Paine and Co., than the Church to the teachings of Christ — but we will not raise it.

After a number of such ultimatums as those we have quoted, His Pseudolency devotes some pages to the *devils* of history. It is here that the Mephisto part of him takes the reins.

Through these pages there is the most eloquent, powerful and, as I may say, exhaustive defense of "the devils" that has ever been made this side of their place of general rendezvous — the lecturer seems to make this a sort of peroration to his former discourse, and hence its eloquence; he speaks as a minister and envoy with full authority, and hence its power; he makes a personal matter of it, and hence it is entirely exhaustive. It has been said: a man is never so strong as when fighting for his own fireside; never so eloquent as when defending his family history.

It is here that he utters those remarkable words with which he adorns his title-page: " Banish me from Eden when you will," etc. But they do not stand alone here, as there — he prefaces them — paves the way to their acceptance, as it were. Hear what an elo-

quent and touching appeal he makes in this
glowing picture of the elder Mephisto.

"If the account given in Genesis is really
true, ought we not, after all, to thank this ser-
pent? He was the first schoolmaster, the first
advocate of learning, the first enemy of ignorance, the first to whisper in human ears the
sacred word of liberty, the creator of ambition,
the author of modesty, of inquiry, of doubt, of
investigation, of progress, and of civilization."

It is just after he has delivered himself of
this, while standing off and regarding the
masterpiece of his art—this matchless pen-
portrait of his patron and hero, that he
breaks loose from himself, lets go all holds, so
to speak, and gives vent to the "Give me the
storm and tempest" business.

Ah, "what a piece of work is man!"—but
here we must end the quotation—we might,
however, add the "how infinite in faculties"
part of it, for if there ever was an evidence
of wonderful "faculties," we have it here.
O tempora! O mores!—Oh, pshaw!

After this Herculean effort, His Pseudolency takes up the thought with which he opened his lecture. Why he dropped it so suddenly before, can only be accounted for, perhaps, (as a like style of procedure prevails all through the book,) from the fact that he has no regular gait — simply plungeth where he listeth and thou seest the dust thereof but canst not tell whence he cometh or whither he goeth, and, may we not conclude, "so is every one that is born of the" — devil?

The first sentence of his lecture, which we have already given, it will be remembered, was as follows : " Each nation has created a god," etc. The one with which he renews the thought on page twenty-six (26) runs after this fashion : " Nothing can be plainer than that each nation gives to its god its peculiar characteristics, and that every individual gives to his god his personal peculiarities." He continues : " Man has no ideas and can have none, except those suggested by his surroundings. He cannot conceive of anything utterly unlike what he has seen or felt," etc. And so he

goes on in his philosophical semi-plagiarisms.
But I have less fault to find with these bor-
rowed scraps of wisdom than the ultimatum
with which he follows them. It is, surely, as
illogical a sequence as he could have possibly
blundered into. Here it is :

" Beyond nature man cannot go even in
thought ; above nature he cannot rise ; below
nature he cannot fall."

Now suppose that instead of this *pot-pourri*
we should substitute the following :

Man has no ideas, and can have none, except those that are founded in fact, (this is,
virtually, the boiling down of His Pseudolency's *pot*, after the impurities have been
skimmed off,) — which, once admitted, this
follows :

Man can, therefore, conceive of nothing
which does not, in some form or degree, exist.
Again :

Man can aspire to nothing of which he has
no conception. The existence of aspiration,
therefore, necessarily implies conception ; conception necessarily implies being — fact.

Man's one supreme aspiration is immortality and eternal life — *heaven ;* therefore the existence of heaven is a *fact.*

So, as I say, I have little fault to find with Mr. Ingersoll's apparent plagiarisms ; it is to his sequences that I object.

The author, next, takes occasion to offer an abridged commentary on the fourth chapter of St. Matthew, which I will give, as it is quite brief, quotation included :

" Then was Jesus led up of the spirit into the wilderness to be tempted of the devil. And when the tempter came to Him, he said : If thou be the Son of God command that these stones be made bread. But he answered and said : It is written, Man shall not live by bread alone, but by every word that proceedeth out of the mouth of God !

" Then the devil taketh Him up into the holy city, and setteth Him upon a pinnacle of the temple, and saith unto Him : If thou be the Son of God, cast thyself down, for it is written, He shall give His angels charge concerning thee, lest at any time thou dash thy

foot against a stone. Jesus said unto him :
It is written again, Thou shalt not tempt the
Lord thy God. Again the devil taketh him
up into an exceeding high mountain and show-
eth him all the kingdoms of the world and the
glory of them, and saith unto him : All these
will I give thee if thou wilt fall down and worship me."

Here are Mr. Ingersoll's comments :

" The Christians now claim that Jesus was
God. If he was God, of course the devil
knew that fact, and yet according to this
account, the devil took the omnipotent God
and placed Him upon a pinnacle of the temple,
and endeavored to induce Him to dash Himself against the earth.   Failing in that, he
took the Creator, owner and governor of the
universe, up into an exceeding high mountain
and offered him this world — this grain of sand
— if He, the God of all the worlds, would fall
down and worship him, a poor devil, without
even a tax title to one foot of dirt ! Is it possible the devil was such an idiot ? Should any
great credit be given to this Deity for not

being caught with such chaff? Think of it! The devil, the prince of sharpers, the king of cunning, the master of finesse, trying to bribe God with a grain of sand that belonged to God! Is there in all the religious literature of the world anything more grossly absurd than this?"

Again, I say, oh, Prince of Pusillanimous Pettifoggers! that could put in *print* such a construction as this; for how can it be possible that so brilliant a man *could* have been so stupid?

Yet, with that charity for ignorance which I have often demanded, no doubt, on my own behalf, I will proceed for the time being upon the presumption that His Pseudolency was innocently in earnest, and give what I have always supposed to be the very common-sense acceptance of the passage in question.

Christ allegorically represents, here, humanity in three different stages or conditions, each subject to the temptations of evil according to his place or condition.

In the first, He personates that unfortunate

class who, unprovided with the necessities of life, are tempted to seek the means of physical existence through other than the proper channels. To these the lesson is found in the answer He gives: "Man shall not live by bread alone, but by every word that proceedeth out of the mouth of God."

In the second, Christ symbolizes those who are tempted to *test*, as a matter of simple experiment, the promises of God. To these He would say, "Thou shalt not tempt the Lord thy God."

In the third, He typifies those who, by virtue of superior abilities, are capable of rising to power and place, and who are tempted to secure these ends even at the cost of their own souls. The lesson is a very suggestive one. To these He would say, "Entertain the thought not for a single moment; there is more danger of your falling than all others"; or, in the words of the answer given, to such a tempter say, "Get thee hence, Satan!"

That this entire passage is simply figurative, and was intended as nothing else, is demon-

strated in the thought of seeing all the kingdoms of the world from an exceeding high
mountain. *Literally* considered, it would have
required an *exceeding* high mountain, sure
enough, from which to take in so extensive a
view.

Now, I am not a preacher (this is, however,
no doubt, quite evident), nor have I opportunity, perhaps I should say inclination, to
consult the commentators, and so I don't
know whether this is an orthodox version or
not, nor do I care ; but it strikes me as being
pre-eminently common - sense - odox, and I'll
chance it.

[I am tempted here to borrow another brace
of Dr. Holmes' brackets; and as the good Doc-
tor has plenty to spare, I think I shall do so,
just to drop in two little items apropos of two
of the three answers given by Christ in the
quotations we have cited. Here they are:

I think that the one I have numbered " second " has especial application to, and includes
excellent advice for, Mr. Tyndall in relation to
his " prayer test."

The "third" may be studied with possible good effect by the gifted and accomplished hero of this paper.]

Immediately following this dissertation on the temptation, our author favors us with the following:

"These devils, according to the Bible, were of various kinds; some could. speak and hear, others were deaf and dumb. All could not be cast out in the same way. The deaf and dumb spirits were quite difficult to deal with. St. Mark tells us of a gentleman who brought his son to Christ. The boy, it seems, was possessed of a dumb spirit, over which the disciples had no control. Jesus said unto the spirit, I charge thee come out of him, and enter no more into him! Whereupon the deaf spirit (having heard what was said) cried out (being dumb) and immediately vacated the premises."

Now, for profoundness of stupidity, and absolute metaphysical idiocy, I challenge the world to show anything that will compare with that! It is, positively, a disgrace and slander upon the intelligence of Infidelity (for Mr.

Ingersoll holds a position as the greatest Infidel of his country) that such a construction
as this should get into print. *Need* I explain
the text? Yes, for His Pseudolency's sake,
for I see· by my morning's paper that he re-
peats it in his lecture in New York. I would
not insult an intelligent reader by deeming it
necessary.

Know, then, oh, Prince of commentators,
that it was simply the *boy* who was dumb, not
the *spirit* that *caused* the affliction. For all
we know, *that* evil spirit may have had the
power of hearing and speaking, even to as
subtle purpose as yourself. We may be *as-
sured* of this much : that he knew who was
talking to him, and *obeyed*, as any sensible
devil would do under the circumstances,— did
not lift up his puny strength in rebellion. Let
this serve us all as a valuable lesson !

But even granting, as you put it, that it was
the evil spirit that was deaf and dumb, and
not the boy, do you not realize that the power
that was able to deliver the boy of his in-
firmity, i. e., cast out the devil, was sufficient to

2*

give hearing and speech to the devil He cast out? Oh, what a precious mess you have made of it!

Our author devotes the next twenty pages of his work to a discussion of cause and effect. All readers are conversant with what he offers here, and have been for many years ; he brings nothing new.

It would be tedious to follow him through the throes of his struggle — his plunging and bellowing as he starts off at full speed, first in the beaten track of one herd, then in another, then, retracing his steps to start on a third, then breaking across paths ; crashing through forests, and pawing the beautiful grasses and flowers that have been gathering their strength and glory for years. No ; we will not try to follow him where he loses himself again and again — in the jungles where many sincere and earnest men have been for-ever lost — in the dark and gloomy and end-less caverns of doubt — the unfathomable depths of the mysterious — the limitless heights of the unknown ! We will wait, and he will soon return to the place whence he started; for he is lost, and goes ever round and round!

Ah! he is already here! And now we shall hear what he says, for though it is not new it is unique.

" Thought is a form of force. We walk with the same force with which we think. Man is an organism, that changes several forms of force into thought force. Man is a machine, into which we put what we call food, and produce what we call thought. Think of that wonderful chemistry by which bread was changed into the divine tragedy of Hamlet."

It will be observed in this passage, as in all that His Pseudolency is pleased to write or speak, there is no apparent evidence of humility. He deals entirely in ultimatums. *Suus cuique mos*, and this is his. It is to be hoped that he will outgrow this, but the prospect is, certainly, not flattering.

The question which he disposes of here so summarily, I need hardly state, is one with which the greatest minds have been struggling

for centuries ; the brightest lights of his own
philosophical household — his very household
gods, as it were — have trembled in the presence of the awful responsibility of pronouncing
upon it ; and yet, with all the assurance of a
mountebank, this man simply waves his quill
in air, it poises but a moment, descends, traces
a few brief lines on the page, and lo ! the mystery of mysteries is solved !

Through all the years of the past, in which
scientists have wrestled with fact and philosophy, the principle involved here has ex-
hausted the highest resources of all schools.
In this struggle have been numbered the
brightest geniuses and most profound philosophers, the astute scholars of the world.
Honest, sincere, noble, genuine men have
devoted their lives to the solution of this one
great problem that underlies all others.

It has appeared in a multitude of forms,
and has been considered from as many different standpoints.

It is presented here in its latest form, which
resolves itself into this :

Whether the action of the brain causes thought, or whether *thought,* an extraneous something which we cannot comprehend, causes the action of the brain.

But the clouds which so long obscured the horizon of faith have, at last, been dispelled by the sunlight of science, thank God, and now we may walk out in the morning of the glorious day! The path is very plain and very simple. We have only to *start* right, and then keep straight ahead. Truths that are of most value are usually expressed in simplest form; they are seldom found in the labyrinthine depths of indefinite metaphysics.

Now, had Mr. Ingersoll even consulted the very primer of science, he would have found, standing out prominently, as the first letter of its alphabet, this incontrovertible truth — *Matter is inert.*

Had he taken the trouble to consult Prof. Bain, who is the acknowledged leader of the most recent school of materialists, — a school which embraces the acute scholars and brightest minds of that philosophy — he would have found even him admitting that matter is inert and cannot *originate* force.

Had he read a little farther in his primer he would have found that there are but two things in the universe — *matter* and *mind.*

It would have required but a very gentle exercise of his reasoning faculties to show him that since matter is *inert* and cannot *originate* force or motion, and *mind* is the only other existence *in* the universe, force or motion must emanate from *mind.*

And then he could, surely, have endured the further mental effort necessary to show him that (as he had already committed himself to the proposition that *thought* is a form of force) *thought* must emanate from *mind*, not matter, or bread, as he puts it.

And all this without going beyond the very primer of science.

It is by no means sure, however, that he would have had the honesty to confess to the truth of that which we have shown here, simple as it is. Now, as I have already stated, I usually accord to *all* men honesty of purpose, but

I fear we must make an exception here, and also in the very next point he seeks to make, for it could not have been a lack of mental acumen (for Mr. Ingersoll is as brilliant a man as there is on the continent) which prompted him, on the page following the quotation I have given, to start out to prove that "matter, force, law, order, cause and effect, exist without a being superior to nature" in the way that he does. Here are his words:

"Now, *suppose* that two atoms should come together, would there be an effect? Yes." From this he makes to follow, law, order, etc. It will be observed that his "suppose" brings about an effect without a *cause*, which is scientifically impossible. Of course *if* two atoms should come together, all else that he claims would follow; but that which is embraced in the little word *if*, or his "suppose," is *just what is in controversy.*

It were easy to demolish the entire super-structure which he so artfully puts together in the pages that follow here,— for it all stands upon the same foundation, this same "sup-

pose," this same little *if* with which he started,— by the application of the two simple
lessons we have referred to from the little
first primer of Science; for scientific truth
is as relentless as it is merciless and powerful, and the two little dynamic atoms in our
possession would reduce his rickety old mu-
seum of nondescript curiosities to a mass of
worthless débris in short order.

To those who have not had the honor of a
personal acquaintance with Mr. Ingersoll, the
wonder is, no doubt, that a man of his apparent erudition in other directions should be so
grossly ignorant of the very first principles of
science, and still have the audacity to send
out a volume involving so many scientific
theories.   Not so, however, with any one who
may know him.

He is a nineteenth century Lawyer and the
paragon of Advocates ; of massive brain, of
brilliant wit, of incomparable *repartee.*   He is
acute but not accurate, wise but not learned,
great but not god-like ; with an entire absence
of *special* knowledge he dons the garb of a

philosophe with admirable skill, for he possess-
es tact, talent and tenacity, and is unfettered
by men, methods, or modesty. He is more
powerful on the rostrum than on paper,—
better suited to the arena than the library or
boudoir. He is a master of trick and of ora-
tory; indeed, in this, I think he is without a
peer in America. He has a quaint style of
putting his sentences, which gives them a peculiar attraction; and so he is quite popular
with the masses, particularly so with those
who would live without the restraint of law —
his very audacity, with this class, is a commen-
dation.

But, really, I must beg pardon — I did
not intend to become his biographer. I am
rather disposed to laughter, and when I
find him urging with so much eloquence that
" Man is a machine into which we put what
we call food and produce what we call
thought," I cannot help the reflection, what a
great pity it is that we were not all *crammed*
in our youth.

We have but to turn a page or two farther

3

to find that Mr. Ingersoll makes an admission
that is fatal to his entire philosophy. I will
quote the verse complete, for I desire to give
him the full force of connections.

" Nature, so far as we can discern, without
passion and without intuition, forms, trans-
forms, and retransforms forever. She neither
weeps nor rejoices. She produces man without purpose, and obliterates him without re-
gret. She knows no distinction between the
beneficial and the hurtful. Poison and nutrition, pain and joy, life. and death, smiles and
tears are alike to her. She is neither merci-
ful nor cruel. She cannot be flattered by
worship nor melted by tears. She does not
know even the attitude of prayer. She appreciates no difference between poison in the
fangs of snakes and mercy in the hearts of
men. *Only through Man does nature take
cognizance of the good, the true, and the beautiful;* and, so far as we know, man is the
highest intelligence."

The sentence I have put in italics — *only
through Man does nature take cognizance of*

the good, the true, and the beautiful — is not italicised in the original. With this exception I have given it just as it appears there. Now I propose to let it remain, just as it is, without comment, or analysis, or any word of mine whatever.

And there it stands! — a monument of truth, looking down upon the· débris of error that is all about it! There it stands! Kissing the sunlight of its higher, purer atmosphere, while malarious contagion broods round its base! There it stands! in solitary grandeur, hero and conqueror, in the very midst of the battle-field, while the self-slain legions of error strew, everywhere, the plain!

Let us carve an inscription upon it — an inscription that has graced the monuments of many battle-fields before.

> "Truth crushed to earth will rise again,
>   The immortal years of God are hers!
> But Error, wounded, writhes in pain
>   And dies amid her worshipers."

A careful observer will notice that it is seldom the case but that in every controversy Truth will assert herself. Was there

ever an instance where she was more sig-
nally successful than here? I have never
known one. It was easily done — the means
of Truth are usually simple. His Pseudolency was merely allowed to *proceed*, and
the Minotaur part of him got the advantage
of the Mephisto part of him, and as he
went plunging and bellowing and roaring
through the fields of philosophy, he fell
over one of the corner-stones of science that
I spoke of a while ago.

Hic jacet Ingersoll — His Pseudolency has
more lives than a cat. Before we can finish
his epitaph, we find him up again and lashing
his sides with redoubled fury. How he roars,
as he pronounces the following:

"Would an infinite, wise, good and powerful God, intending to produce man, commence
with the lowest possible forms of life, with the
simplest organisms that can be imagined, and
during innumerable periods of time, slowly
and almost imperceptibly improve upon the
rude beginning, until man was evolved?
Would countless ages thus be wasted in the

production of awkward forms, afterward aban-
doned ? "

Well, what would Mr. Ingersoll say to this ?
It strikes me that these questions would be
more pertinent if directed to an Infidel. I am
unacquainted with any form of Christianity
that holds to the evolution theory of creation,
so far as *man* is concerned.

The god which His Pseudolency paws and
bellows around so threateningly is not the
Christian's God ; it is the boasted god of the
Infidels. It will be discovered, here, that our
Minotaur has simply lost all control of himself, in his rage, and, not observing that he has
got on the wrong side of the philosophical
fence, he is goring his own god and tearing
up his own plantation.

Hear him again ; he is becoming very ferocious :

" What would we think of a father who
should give a farm to his children, and, before
giving them possession, should plant upon it
thousands of deadly shrubs and vines ; should
stock it with ferocious beasts and poisonous

reptiles; should take pains to put a few
swamps in the neighborhood to breed ma-
laria; should so arrange matters that the
ground would occasionally open and swallow
a few of his darlings, and besides all this,
should establish a few volcanoes in the immediate vicinity, that might at any moment
overwhelm his children with rivers of fire.
Suppose that this father neglected to tell
his children which of the beasts were deadly;
that the reptiles were poisonous; and kept
the volcano business a profound secret; would
we pronounce him angel, or fiend?"

Now, let us admit, for the while, that His
Pseudolency is right in maintaining that there
is no such a being as the Christian God— the
natural state of the world, which he has very
accurately pictured as a farm, is still the same.
This is no catch-logic, it is a fair proposition.

Mr. Ingersoll's entire effort in his lecture is
to prove that the Christian God is a myth; or,
in other words, that there is no such a being,
and sets up, instead, his god of Reason, whatever that may be, as the author and finisher

of all things. He then gives a very graphic and *correct* description of the world as we find it; it follows, therefore, that the "infinite fiend" who created the world is Mr. Ingersoll's god of Reason. This is the only logical deduction.

There is but one way by which Mr. Ingersoll can save his god from the anathema he hurls here, and that is in the theory that the world was created by chance. He will hardly espouse this; the Mephisto part of him is too cunning to permit it.

Behold, then, our Minotaur at bay! Nothing is left to him now but to lash his sides and paw the dust and foam in impotent rage. While he is thus employed, let us have a little talk to ourselves, *for while Mr. Ingersoll is silenced he is not answered.*

The world *is* full of "deadly shrubs and vines, and ferocious beasts, and poisonous reptiles, and malarious swamps, and volcanoes," and millions of other agents of death that Mr. Ingersoll does not name. Nay, even we are ourselves destroyers.

Every moment of our existence is at the expense of myriads of other existences.

A million lives are sacrificed that I may finish this line.

And yet we call our God a God of infinite mercy, tenderness and love.

How shall we reconcile this?

This is the great stumbling-block of Christians — Christians who think just enough to get *into* a mystery without thinking enough to get out.

And this is the perpetual sneer of Skeptics, and the taunt of the Infidels. Let us see if we may not meet the issue fairly, and dispose of it fairly and conclusively. If we do this we are consistent Christians; if we do not, we are inconsistent. A man is worse than a coward who would dodge this question — he is a suicide. There is no one so contemptible as he who willingly deceives himself. Oh, what a hollow mockery is that faith that is founded upon a lie!

I desire to say, right here, that no society, religious or otherwise, or any person or persons whomsoever, save and except myself, are either directly or indirectly responsible for the position I am about to assume.

I hold then :

First. The laws of the physical universe, just as they exist, are the only *possible* laws to the physical.

Second. The laws of the spiritual universe, just as they exist, are the only *possible* laws to the spiritual.

Third. The conditions of life and death, pleasure and pain, etc., as pertaining to the physical, and the conditions of happiness and grief, etc., as pertaining to the spiritual, are the positive and negative poles, abso-lutely necessary, respectively to physical and spiritual existence.

I shall endeavor to sustain these three propositions from a purely scientific stand-point, and by strict, logical method.

In relation, then, to our first proposition, that the laws of the physical universe, just as they exist, are the only *possible* laws to the physical, I desire to offer :

First. That bed-rock of scientific truth, Matter, is indestructible.

Second. If matter is indestructible, it follows that matter must always exist.

Third. If matter must always exist, it follows that matter can have no end.

Fourth. If matter can have no end, it follows that matter could have had no beginning. Since that which has a beginning must have an end. Since that which has no beginning can have no end. An axiom.

Fifth. If matter had no beginning and can have no end, it follows that the laws which govern matter had no beginning and can have no end. Since the law which governs must be co-existent with the thing governed.

Sixth. If the laws which govern matter had no beginning and can have no end, it follows that the laws which govern matter (or the physical), are the only laws *possible* to the physical, as claimed in our *First* proposition.

In relation to our second proposition, respecting the spiritual universe, the same method need only be pursued in order to establish it.

We will begin with that other bed-rock of scientific truth : *Mind* is indestructible.

You know the scientists tell us that there are but two things that exist in the universe, —*matter* and *mind*—that the first is *inert*, but that both are indestructible. That is why I call the two principles I have given the bed-rock principles — or the two principles that underlie all others.

To establish then, our second proposition, we will begin :

First. Mind is indestructible.

Second. If mind is indestructible, it follows that mind (by which we mean the spiritual) must always exist.

Third. If mind must always exist, it follows that mind can have no end.

Fourth. If mind can have no end, it follows that mind could have had no beginning, since that which has a beginning must have an end,— since that which has no beginning can have no end. An axiom.

Fifth. If mind had no beginning, and can have no end, it follows that the laws which govern mind (or the spiritual) had no beginning, and can have no end,— since the law which governs must be co-existent with the thing governed.

Sixth. If the laws which govern mind (or the spiritual) had no beginning, and can have no end, it follows that the laws which govern mind (or the spiritual) are the only laws *possible* to the spiritual, as claimed in our *second* proposition.

I think we may reach these two conclusions from another standpoint—the idea of God-ship. By God we mean the Supreme Being, and, as in the Persian *Goda* or *Khoda*, we imply by the word God the idea of lord, master, ruler. The qualities absolutely necessary *to* Godship are those of omniscience, omnipresence, and omnipotence. No doubt we shall all agree in this.

Well, if God existed prior to matter or the identity of other existences, of what *could* he have been omniscient? Wherein *could* he

have been omnipresent? Over whom or
what *could* he have been omnipotent? Or, in
other words, how could he have been omniscient of nothing, omnipresent nowhere, omnipotent over nobody? Or, with the simple
meaning of the very word God, how could he
be lord, master, or ruler over nothingness?

Clearly, then, since God had no beginning,
and can have no end, mind had no beginning,
and can have no end, and matter had no beginning, and can have no end; and therefore
the laws that govern mind and matter had no
beginning, and can have no end. Since the
laws that govern must be co-existent with the
thing governed, they are, therefore, the only
possible laws *to* Spiritual and Physical existence.

It may be well to drop in, right here, an
additional scientific truth, lest our Pseudo-
Divinity-Doctors shall throw up their hands
in holy horror, realizing that if everything
that has a beginning must have an end, *man*
having had a beginning, according to their
theology, must have an end. Here it is ·

Man was made of the two already existing
materials — *matter*, which the Bible speaks of
as " dust of the earth," and *mind*, which the
Bible calls " breath of life "; these two had no
beginning, and can have no end; therefore
man had no beginning, and can have no end,
the body being a part of matter, and the
soul being a part of God.

[We cannot pause to discuss the distinc-
tions of mind and soul or spirit, the relations
of body and soul, or the relations of soul to
God after the soul has been granted a separate, individual identity by God ; that must remain for another time ; though all this may be
logically demonstrated.]

Before passing to our *third* proposition, I
wish to apply the first two to the subject before us.

Now, if we have established those two propositions, it will be seen that *responsibility* for
the laws of physical and spiritual existence
rests not with God, but in the very necessities
to physical and spiritual existence.   Or, to be
plainer, what Mr. Ingersoll refers to as deadly

shrubs and vines, and ferocious beasts, and poisonous reptiles, and malarious swamps, and the millions of other agents of death, are not chargeable to the malignity of a creator, but to the *absolute necessities.*

The truth of this will become only the more apparent after the consideration of our *third* proposition, which was as follows :

The conditions of life and death, pleasure and pain, etc., as pertaining to the physical, and the conditions of happiness and grief, etc., as pertaining to the spiritual, are the positive and negative poles, absolutely necessary respectively to physical and spiritual existence.

Now the poverty of our language compels me to explain what I mean by the *positive and negative poles* — a figure I have taken from electrics — and *in* the explanation I think I shall establish our proposition.

I shall endeavor to be very plain and simple, for the plainest, simplest language is always the strongest and most convincing. And we may also be very brief in this. By *positive and negative poles*, then, in the con-

nection I have used them, as absolute necessities, I mean what geometricians imply when
they speak of two lines as necessary to a parallel; what Prof. Cook implies when he says
that there cannot be an over without an
under, a higher without a lower, an inner
without an outer, a hither without a yonder.

It is as *inconceivable* that pleasure should
exist without the *possibility* of pain, or that
happiness should exist without the *possibility*
of grief, as that a parallel should exist without
the second line; or that you can have an over
without an under, a higher without a lower,
an inner without an outer, a hither without a
yonder. Each takes its place in the list of
absolute necessities. And so we might continue in the realms of matter and mind,
*throughout which we can find nothing without
its opposite.* And MAN, compelled to move in
a given direction, would simply be propelled
as an inanimate. In other words: if it were
impossible for man to move except in the
straight line of *good,* he would be, and *could
be,* no more than the tree that springs up

from the earth as a blade of grass, grows to the perfection of maturity buds, blooms bears its fruit, and then dies, to go back to the elements.

Now, we may lay down two broad principles here as the logical sequence of our former propositions; and while we need hold no school of physicists and no school of philoso-phers responsible, we, at the same time, may challenge disproval. Here they are:

First. There is not an *atom* in the physical universe which is absolute, i. e., entirely in-dependent of all other atoms.

Second. There is not a *condition* in the spirit-ual universe which is absolute, i. e., entirely independent of all other conditions.

It will be observed that I have not yet dis-posed of the conditions of life and death to the physical, of our *third* proposition and it will be remembered that I numbered these as with the absolute necessities. Let us con-sider them:

From the standpoint of science, life and death are but the processes of re-creation in

3*

which death is as absolutely necessary as the
first line of a parallel; consequently, from a
scientific point of view, there is no loss, the
new life compensating for the old death.

This pertains to the animal, vegetable, and
mineral kingdoms, and, according to science,
has always done so — the law being co-existent
with the thing governed. The responsibility,
therefore, rests not with God, but with the .
necessities to being.

Besides, I challenge the *possibility* of a *conception* of being other than this. For that
would involve the making of something out of
nothing, and, as Mr. Ingersoll has pertinently
remarked, " Nothing, considered in the light of
a raw material, is a most decided failure."

But you will say here, how do you reconcile
this with the Bible account of creation ? I
answer, by the Bible itself. You will reply that
the Bible says: " In the beginning God created the heavens and the earth." (Now bear
in mind it is you who have opened the Bible,
not I.) I reply, the Bible says no such thing.
You contend that it does, and show me the

text of a King James translation. I then refer you to the original, if you are a Hebrew
scholar; if not, I commend you to any Hebrew
brew scholar in whom you may have confi
dence. Ask him to translate the Hebrew
text for you into simple English. He will
tell you that the first verse is very difficult to
translate accurately into our language, and
show you the peculiarities of the Hebrew.
He will tell you that the Anglo-Saxon words
which most correctly embody the meaning are
as follows :

First verse : In this beginning God rearranged
the heavens and the earth.

Second verse : For the earth had been wrecked
and desolated.

Now you may ask, Why was it not translated so in the King James text? Probably
for the same reason that they were so in-
accurate in many other places. You know
that they translated from the Greek, which
was itself a translation from the Hebrew.
And you will perhaps remember the experiment that was tried a few years ago, of

passing a simple English sentence through half a dozen different languages, and then back into English. Its author would have never recognized it.

This that is given here is the correct translation, *and it is as old as Polycarp and St. Augustine.*

But you will say: Back of this beginning there must have been the former earth and other worlds. Very correct! Matter has always existed, and God has always existed, and as He put this world together from already existing material, so has He put other worlds together.

The best way is, I think, to make it a principle to accept a *fact* wherever it may come from ; and if, like a streak of lightning, it crashes into our " metin'-house," go to work to repair the damages, and make things light-ning-proof for the future.

Now I do not consider that I am called upon to believe anything simply because it is in the Bible, but because it is *true.* It is not true merely because it is in the Bible, but it is in the Bible because it *is* true; *and that is why there is nothing in the Bible that is not true.*

By substituting this for the King James version, the first chapter of Genesis correctly understood will be found to be in entire harmony with the teachings of Science, and the most accurate and wonderful piece of epitomized history that can be found in the literature of the world.

When Mr. Ingersoll proclaims that there is an irrepressible conflict between Science and Christianity, he is but repeating a declaration that was made years ago when ignorance, like a pall of universal right, enveloped the world. There is yet a sort of conflict which is kept up between certain scientists and a few ignorant, though, no doubt, well-meaning theologians; but there is *no* conflict between Science and Christianity, and the day is not far distant when science will be universally recognized, as it is already in the higher schools of philosophy and advanced theology, as the hand-maid of Christianity.

This is no idle boast, but as sure as that
to morrow's dawn will supersede the night.

But now our Minotaur is ready for another
charge ; he has partially recovered from his
recent defeat, and is preparing to renew the
attack.   Listen to him :

" Here empires may be overthrown ; dynas-
ties may be extinguished in blood ; millions
of slaves may toil 'neath the fierce rays of
the sun and the cruel strokes of the lash ;
yet all is happiness in heaven.   Pestilences
may strew the earth with corpses of the
loved ; the survivors may bend above them
in agony, yet the placid bosom of heaven is
unruffled.   Children may expire vainly asking
for bread ; babes may be devoured by ser-
pents, while gods sit smiling in the clouds.
The innocent may languish unto death in ob-
scurity of dungeons ; brave men and heroic
women may be changed to ashes at the
bigot's stake, while heaven is filled with
songs of joy.   Out on the wild sea, in dark-
ness and in storm, the shipwrecked struggle
with the cruel waves, while angels play upon

their golden harps. . . . In heaven they are too happy to have sympathy, too busy singing to aid the imploring and destitute. Their eyes are blinded; their ears are stopped, and their hearts are turned to stone by the infinite selfishness of joy. . . . The smiles of the deities are unacquainted with the tears of men. The shouts of heaven drown the sobs of earth."

What there is here of fact, so far as the laws of nature are concerned, I have already answered at some length in the preceding pages; what remains of *fiction* I will now notice briefly.

It will be observed that our Minotaur is still so blinded by his impotent rage that he knows not his own. He charges here through the Infidel heaven, paws up its Infidel streets, and butts down its Infidel walls; makes war upon the Infidel angels, and gores the Infidel god.

For the *Christian* heaven is a heaven wherein there is more joy over one that is saved than over ninety and nine that went

not astray. For the *Christian* angels are
they that minister continually unto the children of men. For the *Christian* God is One
who so loved the world that He gave His
only begotten Son that whosoever believeth
in Him should not perish but have everlasting life.

Mr. Ingersoll devotes the remainder of
his lecture to prophecy, in which he predicts
the downfall of the Christian system, and
supports his position by arguing that as all
the religions of the barbarous ages have
fallen into ruin, so must the religion of the
Christian age.

Now, this may be good enough Infidel
logic, but it is not the logic of common
sense, not even of very common sense.

Because systems founded in error and ignorance have failed, therefore, a system founded in truth and knowledge *must* fail? Surely,
the Mephisto part has retired; this is too
stupid to be cunning; it is entirely Mino-
taurian.

Oh, massive-fronted Ingersoll! Verily, and

of a truth, great is Reason, and great is Ingersoll, her prophet ! Selah !

We come now to the peroration. But His
Pseudolency makes an entire new departure
in the way of rhetorical construction. He
puts his peroration right in the middle of
his discourse, and so we must go back to
consider it. Of course he has both the legal
and constitutional right, if he chooses, to do
so. I simply make the allusion as a sort of
landmark in my survey.

Here is the passage referred to :

" The church wishes us to believe. Let the
church, or one of its intellectual saints, perform a miracle, and we will believe. . . .
We have had talk enough. We have listened
to all the drowsy, idealess, vapid sermons that
we wish to hear. We have read your Bible
and the works of your best minds. We have
heard your prayers, your solemn groans, and
your reverential amens. All these amount
to less than nothing. We want one fact ;
we beg at the doors of your churches for
just one little fact. We pass our hats along

4

your pews and under your pulpits, and im-
plore you for just one fact. We know all
about your mouldy wonders and your stale
miracles. We want a this year's fact. We
want only one. Give us one fact for charity."

Now, notwithstanding the ludicrous spec-
tacle of an Infidel calling for a *fact*, while the
entire system of infidelity is founded in
negation, still, as "it is the breathing time of
day with me," I will endeavor to satisfy His
Pseudolency, and give him that for which he
so melodramatically pleads.

As I before remarked, this perorative appeal
was made in the middle of his lecture, before
he had lashed himself into such a fury, when
the Minotaur part took entire control,— so
that it is the Mephisto part that suggests this
—it is not without cunning.

No doubt His Pseudolency communed with
himself something after this fashion : Now
facts are as old as creation itself. I will call
for a *new fact* which is at once *impossible*.
Again, the Christian God has expressly for-
bidden that His children should *test* Him, for

the test's sake. I will, therefore, demand of
them a miracle. They can comply with
neither and I shall have made my point.

So this appeal is not altogether without
subtlety, and Mr. Ingersoll, no doubt, felt that
it was profoundly cunning. Yet, I think, in the
hypothesis we have just offered of the cerebral
activity of its author, he is fully answered.

But I shall, nevertheless, endeavor to supply what seems so necessary to our hero's happiness. And, since a new fact must be attended with a miracle, I shall offer evidence of the
existence of both at the same time. Indeed
the nineteenth century fact and miracle that I
am about to refer to, form a sort of mystic
dualty — a one in two and two in one, as it
were. And here it is : *His Pseudolency himself—Mephisto-Minotaurus.*

That the continued existence of this man is
a *fact*, no one will deny. That the *continuation* of that existence is the result of nothing
less than a miracle, I will now demonstrate
scientifically, by *special* method.

"Ἵνα τί γέλοιον εἰπῶ κἀι περί γελοίου πράγματος.
Give me leave to be merry on a merry subject.

If we will turn, in the *French Dictionaire de Medicine,* to the article entitled *Combustion humaine,* and in Dr. Apjon's *Cyclopedia of Practical Medicine,* to the article entitled *Spontaneous human combustion,* we can at once satisfy ourselves that the human body may undergo such excesses that, in process of time, decomposition will begin of a peculiar character, and to such an extent as to produce spontaneous combustion, and this, too, in the midst of life.

Now, I desire to make no allusion here to His Pseudolency's corporeal part — I am not his physician and could not, therefore, speak with accuracy — but to his spiritual part — his moral and mental being.

It is a principle in science that wherever there is a close affinity between matter and mind, the laws pertaining to each bear an intimate sympathy. This being the case, and our scientists having already discovered a law of spontaneous human combustion, it only remains a matter of time until they shall discover a law of spontaneous mental and moral combustion. I do not mean that there may be a total destruction of the moral and mental faculties, but a sort of disintegration, as it were, in which the *impure* parts will destroy themselves,— what little there is of any value taking its flight to the source from whence it came.

We should not be compelled, in a case of emergency of this kind, to await the slow, plodding progress of the scientists, when so plain a deduction as this is before us, and it is just as well right here, that we *anticipate* the conclusion to which they must inevitably come at last.

It will readily be seen, then, that all that keeps the moral and mental parts of His Pseudolency from spontaneous combustion is a continual working miracle.

For, as Mr. Carlyle said of him before he was born, " Such a combination of logical life with moral death, so universal a denier, both in head and heart, is undoubtedly an emissary of the Primeval Nothing," and we may add, must be for some wise and inscrutable purpose

miraculously permitted an existence from day
to day, since his continued intellectual life is
in violation of every law in the reach of the
scientists.

Such an amalgamation of strength and stupidity, sense and sophistry, axiom and absurd-
ity, intelligence and idiocy, acumen and arro-
gance, genius and drivel, reason and ridicu-
lousness, and then, notwithstanding his royal
good-fellowship, such a compound of unblush-
ing pretension, swaggering insolence, and blas-
phemous sacrilege, as is evinced in the lecture
before us ; in a word, such a mass of intellectual contradictions and moral corruption is an
anomaly in the universe, beyond the pales of
law, and can only be kept together — saved
from spontaneous combustion—by the direct,
daily, hourly interposition of miraculous
power.

His Pseudolency has, therefore, "a this
year's fact," a walking, living, present evidence of " miracle." *Requiescat in pace !*

Why he is thus permitted, were a difficult
problem ; I cannot solve it, unless the solu-

tion be that it is for a similar purpose to that for which we put a light-house on a dangerous coast; that he is *permitted* to warn others of that moral and mental destruction that lurks beneath the waves of Infidelity.

I have endeavored to give a faithful review of every intended point in the lecture of " the gods," and this is the epitome of Mr. Ingersoll's philosophy.

If anything has been omitted it is because it was too obscure for my comprehension. I have endeavored to say nothing to excite your prejudice, or to take advantage of the prejudice already existing against Infidels. I have sought to make an honorable fight of it, and if I may have used a little Greek-fire to meet the poisoned arrows of the enemy, I trust that the exigencies of war will justify me.

And now let us have a little talk to ourselves.

It is a sad truth that many *professed* Christians come very far from *being* Christians.

Do you think that if every professed follower
of Christ had been, indeed, a *true* and *faithful* follower of Christ, such a lecture as the
one we have just reviewed would have ever
been written?

Now, the Infidels watch the life of Christians, and they say, that's Christianity; and
they listen to our ministers, and say, that's
Christian doctrine; and they are often compelled to add: We don't want to emulate
that kind of life, and it is impossible to believe that kind of doctrine.

Mr. Ingersoll makes some telling hits on
many of our practices and much of our
preaching, and there is no use of shutting
our eyes to the fact, and trying to drive
away the remembrance by singing psalms.

*I defy Infidelity to find a single fault in
the teachings of Christ!* They have been
trying to do so for two thousand years and
have not succeeded. It is in the practices
and preaching of those who claim to be Christians that they find the fault.

If there were nothing given to the Infidels

to believe but the pure word of Christ, there would soon be no Infidels in the world.

Now, the great trouble with many of our ministers is that the moment they take up a subject of theology, they lay down the practical common-sense that governs them in everyday life, and the result is, their philosophy flies off in a thousand tangents. And they call this orthodoxy, and the Infidels say they don't want that sort of orthodoxy.

And another trouble is, that when they become identified with some particular sect, they think they ought to cling to the ancient landmarks, no matter how inconsistent they may be, with the tenacity of life itself. Suppose our fathers had acted upon the same principle!

The Christian warfare will always be attended with difficulties so long as we furnish the cudgels for Infidels to batter us over the heads with.

I can recognize no excuse for poor preaching. Oh, what a theme is Christianity. What has it not done for this world?

It found anarchy and barbarism ; it has bestowed order and enlightenment.

It found groveling ignorance and superstition ; it has bestowed knowledge and philosophy.

It found man a vassal and slave ; it has lifted him to a peerage with gods !

It found woman a menial and concubine ; it has lifted her to the sphere of angels !

Do you point me to the achievements of the nations before Christ ; their wondrous proficiency in the arts and sciences ?

I will point you to the wreck and ruin of it all. Do you ask why ? Time has written the answer.

Christianity found the human race unable to rise from the miry clay, staggering and blinded and bewildered, through the horror-strewn gorges of Polytheism ; through the caverns of Doubt and Denial ; through the unillumined defiles of a terrible Dread, groping, groping in the deep, dark valley, surrounded by the ghastly specters of the skeletoned past, while Death, brooding like a

monster vampire over the world, cast everywhere its terrible shadow!

But when the chorus rang out on the world
— "Peace! peace on earth, good will to men,"
our poor humanity took heart.

Slowly and steadily we have marched
through all the centuries; slowly but surely,
step by step, mounting the stair of Christ's
enlightenment.

And now, where once the trackless ocean
rolled, and unknown seas kissed back the sun,
commerce sits smiling in a million sails!

And now, where once was howling wilderness and waste, a million fields glow with the
golden grain! a million homes crown life with
happiness!

And now, where once were unknown haunts
of savage beasts, railroads, the swift arteries
of trade, like a broad net-work spread, and the
chained lightnings, girt about the globe, serve
everywhere men's purposes! The land is
decked with cities, and the land is jeweled
over with churches and with schools!

Nay, we have mounted far beyond these

scenes! Behold! where gleam the countless stars, there stretch the highways of all-con· quering science!

And now, where once were unknown heights, and depths profound, are paths wherein we stroll as erstwhile through our gardens!

Where once were grotesque shapes and heathen deities, now, through the illimitable space, roll worlds innumerable! And these we measure, weigh and analyze, delve in their mines, explore their mountains and plains, bask in the light of their resplendent suns, and dally with their gorgeous, tinted beams!

And soon our souls shall listen to their sweet, celestial harmonies!

For in the center of this universe is throned our God, whence time, as a gentle effluence, is shed through all the worlds!

'Twas He who sent to us His Son, that He might lift us up unto Himself. And He has sworn, even by Himself, since He could by no greater swear, with His great arm uplifted, that He *will* do it! *Hic et ubique!* Yes, here and everywhere! *Here*, on this beautiful bright earth, or in the Pleiades! *Here*, with the loved ones of our hearts, or *there*, where they shall come to us!

Stand out, oh Infidel, beneath the stars! Look up! and when your soul throbs wildly to be free,— throbs till your heart leaps madly in your breast,— throbs till your brain reels, and your whole being quakes,— stifle all thought,—quell every impulse,—*confront* your soul,— declare to *it* there is no God,— then hear its swift, wild screaming *laughter*,— endure its loathing, mocking, terrible recoil as it shall answer back, " Thou Fool! "

To your knees, and crawl for pardon! For I tell thee now, thou rash destroyer of thy soul's dear peace, unless thou shalt its quick forgiveness gain, 'twill hunt thee down!

With sting of thousand scorpions thy con-science will so lash thee through the world, thou shalt seek refuge in the very jaws of death! Aye, and beyond the tomb; for there, all dwarfed and maimed, it shall confront thee! Even as thou hast dwarfed and maimed it here, 'twill meet thee there, con-

front thee face to face! Thou shalt stand
self-accused, self-judged, and go self-haunted
through eternity!

For who can escape the presence of his
soul?

ABSOLUTE NECESSITIES.

The man who in this life can keep the whiteness of his soul is not likely to lose it in any other.

ALEXANDER SMITH.

Truth came once into the world with her Divine Master, and was a perfect shape, most glorious to look on; but when He ascended, and His Apostles after him were laid asleep, then straight arose a wicked race of deceivers, who, as the story goes of the Egyptian Typhon with his conspirators, how they dealt with the good Osiris, took the virgin Truth, hewed her lovely form into a thousand pieces, and scattered them to the four winds. From that time ever since, the sad friends of Truth, such as durst appear, imitating the careful search that Isis made for the mangled body of Osiris, went up and down gathering up limb by limb still as they could find them. We have not yet found them all, nor ever shall do, till her Master's second coming: He shall bring together every joint and member, and shall mould them into an immortal feature of Loveliness and Perfection.

MILTON.

THE ABSOLUTE NECESSITIES.

IT shall be my endeavor in the present paper to confine what shall be offered to very
simple, plain, old-fashioned, hard-fisted *facts*,
and their logical deductions. And if, in doing
so, we shall let a little light into the labyrinthine mysteries of some of the popular the-
ologies, and, by that light, discover that those
dark passages may, after all, be explored, and
even by very ordinary people like ourselves,
let us evermore hold in higher regard those
simple truths that are in the reach of all, though
it should be at the expense of that reverence
which we may have hitherto borne for the in-
fallibility of some of our teachers.

And now let us try to divest ourselves of all
preconceived ideas that may have become a
part of our mental being through early train-
ing or past associations,— all prejudices, so to
speak, that may enswathe us, and upon truths

4*

that we know to be truths — plain, practicable,
common-sense principles of every-day life —
consider the grave question before us, for
" *to this complexion must we come at last.*"

Were we to seek for the cause of the unfortunate tendency of the human mind, particularly as applied to Christians, to veil everything in mystery, we should, no doubt, find it
very largely attributable to a misconstruction
of the idea that lingers around those words
of Holy Writ, " Great are the mysteries of
godliness." The inspired writer might have
added, " Great are the mysteries of germinal
life," but it is, no doubt, well he did not do so,
else who knows but that our agriculturists
would now be exhausting themselves in an effort to raise corn in the hot sands of Arabia,
or on the snow-capped summits of the Alps.

Because there are great mysteries connected
with the raising of corn, it does not follow that
there are not many simple, practical truths
leading *to* the raising of corn. And because
there are great mysteries connected *with* godliness, it does not follow that there are not

many simple, practical truths leading *to* godliness. Nor does it follow that because there
must forever remain many unsolved problems
in eternity, that there are not many simple,
practical truths in connection with that future
state that are within the reach of every rational
mind.

Now, for some little time let us confine our
arguments to limits that will not touch the
Christian system, or the relationship of Christ
to humanity. Let us advance to the consideration of that thought, that sublime climax of
philosophy, by gradual approach, each step of
which shall be as sure as the very foundation
of science. We should do this for two reasons :

First. That we may throw some light upon
that part of our question which seems to per-
plex some of our theologians, and that so
greatly disturbed Mr. Beecher : the condition
of the millions who lived and died before the
Christian era.

Second. That what we shall offer may reach
those who do not accept Christ.

Before taking up our subject from a purely
scientific standpoint, let us seek to reduce it
to *practical* proportions, and consider it from
a practical standpoint by making a personal
application of it.

We will for the present use the words,
Heaven, Hell, Saved and Lost, in their popular significance, reserving the privilege of sup-
plying what we conceive to be their proper
definitions after a while.

I desire now to address the one reader
whose eye may be resting upon this page, for
it is not probable that there is a single individual on the habitable globe but who *feels*
that by some means he or she will be saved.
Indeed it is hardly possible that there could
be found a single instance of one so devoid
of hope as to believe that he would be lost—
that would be despair.   Though unable to
give a reason for the faith that is within, all
feel that, by some means, a way will be pro-
vided through which they will be led to a final
state of happiness.

It is not proposed, at *this* point, to discuss

any doctrines as to qualifications *for*, or to dic-
tate any peculiar individual conception *of*,
heaven. But accepting, in order to pursue
the argument, any rational conception you
may have of heaven, and accepting the idea
of that unbounded goodness of God which
presupposes that He *would* draw all men unto
Himself,— all this conceded, is *your* case a
possible one? What sort of a heaven would
be required to make you happy? You cannot conceive of heaven as other than a state
of purity of soul, where only the highest, holi-
est aspirations may exist, no matter what
other peculiarities you may ally to it,— would
such surroundings make you happy? Were
you at once translated from your present
abode into the presence of God and His
holy angels, could you even endure it?

What sort of a heaven would it take to
satisfy that man whose soul only knows the
greed of gain?

What sort of a heaven would it be wherein
one could feel at home whose chief delight is
in telling or listening to obscene jests?

What sort of a heaven would be required for one whose life is given to the continual gratification of lust ?

You will say, at once, that no one embraced in these extreme cases is a fit subject for the presence of God. And a question arises : What sort of a presence *is* he fitted for ?

How a man can hope for even respectable existence in eternity who allows all manner of unworthy thoughts to take possession of his being ; who permits impurity, with its loathsome associates, to hold a continual high carnival in his soul, is certainly a mystery.

But there are those who believe in a sort of purgatorial repair shop, to work souls over. I do not refer to the Roman Catholics, who have reduced the idea of Purgatory to something less than a science, but to those who have a *feeling* that there will be some kind of purifying process between death and eternity. We will be as generous to these as we were to the others by conceding their premise as a starting-point. It will, then, be admitted, in return, that there are souls so utterly depraved, whom to fit for any rational view of heaven would require an entire destruction of identity. Would not this be equivalent to annihilation ? If, to fit you for God's presence, it becomes necessary to make an entirely new being, it would not be you who would enjoy the heaven, but another — the one newly created.

Well, if this is true in an entire destruction of identity, it must still remain true in a *partial* destruction of identity; for since entire destruction of identity would be equivalent to annihilation, partial destruction of identity would be equivalent to partial annihilation, which is one of the impossibilities.

Let us see if this cannot be made plainer.

Suppose that, in disobedience to physical law, I should thrust my arm under the wheels of a railway engine while it is in motion, my arm would be crushed; suppose a surgeon, to save the rest of my body, should cut the arm off; suppose I should supply its place with a cork arm ; I should not then be the same man physically, but something more than three-fourths of my original self. Suppose, then, I should lose a leg in a similar way, and I should supply its place in a like manner; I should then be a little more than half of my former self, physically. Where would the parts be that were cut away? Destroyed? No; but returned to the elements whence they came originally, for they are indestructible.

Suppose that this process should go on; you can see that I should be all cork, or an entirely new physical being.

Well, after the process was over, which would be the man with which we started? The cork, or those parts that had returned to the elements?

Now the purgatorial repair shop theory is founded upon an idea that the soul may be worked over until it shall be fitted for heaven. Granting the premise and conclusion, I should like to know what becomes of the parts that are cut away. Remember they are indestructible. And if a soul quit this life all dwarfed to the proportions of the hideous deformity

of sin, by what process *could* it be developed
into an acceptable guest at the court of angels
except *by* cutting away the deformed parts so
as to have purity to build upon?

Let us see if this part of the issue may not
be met by pure, scientific method, confining
ourselves to the simplest possible thoughts
and language, and the purest metaphysics.

We will consider a thought from the material world, the world of matter, and one that
we may demonstrate without the aid of the
scientists or theologians. Indeed, we shall be
quite as well off without the assistance of
either of these in this, for the former might
lose us in the labyrinthine depths of their
philosophies, and the latter — well, they are in
a very unsteady state of mind just at present.

Take a piece of polished marble, but scratch
it with a needle and you will have affected it
forever. All the ages of time to come, all the
cycles of eternity, cannot *undo* what you have
done.

True, the scratch may be cut away, and the
surface of the stone may be polished again

5

until it shall again become beautiful, but *it is at the cost of material!* The stone can never be restored to its original proportions. And just in proportion as that piece of marble is affected, whether by the scratch of a needle, the chisel of the sculptor, or the upheaval of a volcano, just to that degree will the effect that is wrought upon it attend it through " the wreck of matter and the crush of worlds."

Now, I hold that a sin, *absolute*, however small, makes an impress on the soul that is eternal in its consequences.

It may be cut away, through forgiveness, and the soul may be perfected by after-life, but there is a *loss* that may never be recovered. And I think this is incontrovertible. Why? Because there are two things which no one will deny, and which no one *can* deny; and those two things are :

First. No one will deny, or can deny, that a life of *continual* sin dwarfs the soul until its possibilities in the future state must be greatly limited.

Second. No one will deny, or can deny, that

this comes not in the *continuation*, for that is without quality, but in the *sin*. *By* continuation comes that enormity of proportion which makes the effect possible to our perception — the sin of a moment being the same in its effect upon the soul with the difference only of degree; and just in proportion as a soul is dwarfed by sin in this life, just to that degree are its possibilities limited in the life to come.

(A stain or soil upon the *marble*, to continue the figure, may be washed away without impairing the proportions of the stone, and there are some offenses ofttimes reckoned sins because of their sinful nature, which but stain or soil the soul, and of these may the soul be cleansed.)

That the future existence of the soul will be surrounded by scenes subject to conditions and capable of possibilities immeasurably beyond its present highest conceptions, is, to my mind, as certain as that the infinite is beyond the finite; *but* that it will be in the precise line, or direction, *of* its aspirations here, seems to me necessary to the deduction, if it remain logical.

Now, I desire to call your attention to the following universally accepted truth:

There are but two states of existence — the here and the hereafter, of time and eternity. And I think that we have demonstrated that just as we quit this life we shall begin the next. I say I think we have demonstrated this to be one of the absolute necessities, for any conclusion different from this must be upon the theory of annihilation, which is one of the impossibilities.

There is another conclusion in connection with the future state that follows from the foregoing arrangement of very simple truths, it is this: There are grades or degrees in the future state. Besides, this is clearly taught in the Bible, and is, I believe, almost universally acknowledged. Now, just one item more, right here: Nothing can be surer than that where there is no law there can be no transgression.

The nations, therefore, that lived before the

coming of Christ could not be amenable to the law of Christ which was made by Christ, and of necessity, after His coming.

It will require no very great amount of mental acumen to see, therefore, that the inhabitants of the world, prior to the Christian era, were only subject to the conditions we have already mentioned, i. e., they began the new life in eternity at the precise point that they ended the old, on earth, save that *there* possibilities became *infinite*, while *here* they were *finite*.

˙ How Mr. Beecher could become so greatly excited, as will appear from the quotation we will give here, over a question that is so entirely beyond all rational controversy is, indeed, remarkable to an extent that becomes incomprehensible to me, upon any hypothesis that would be creditable to a master.

Surely there has been nothing very profound in the simple thoughts we have offered so far, and yet, had they been comprehended in their simplicity by Mr. Beecher, he could have lifted the veil from the great mystery,

the very contemplation of which almost de-
throned his reason, and threw him into such
paroxysms of rhetorical inaccuracy.

' It becomes necessary to quote him here,
that we may not be misunderstood. We shall
take occasion to refer to a passage that comes
before this, after a while ; why I do not take
them as they come is because Mr. Beecher's
erraticisms are secondary considerations to the
argument. I am trying to solve the problem
which is popularly denominated Heaven and
Hell, or the future state, simply disposing
of Beecher-mania as a sort of unknown
quantity wherever it presents itself.

In quoting from Mr. Beecher we are but
quoting the words of a large element of religious and irreligious society, and the thoughts
they suggest are, therefore, by no means
ephemeral.

Referring to the nations before the coming
of Christ, he says :

" If now you tell me that this great mass of
men, because they had not the knowledge of
God, went to heaven, I say the inroad of such

a vast amount of mud swept into heaven would be destructive of its purity, and I cannot accept that view.

"If, on the other hand, you say they went to hell, then you make an Infidel of me. For I do swear" (we will omit the oaths, Mr. Beecher says the reporters were guilty of a — mistake here, that he did not swear. At all events Mr. Beecher shall be allowed to amend). Suffice it that the sentence which follows makes Mr. Beecher very emphatically reject the idea that they went to hell. He fails, however, to tell us where they did go to. Perhaps, according to Beecher-mania, they just went out — vanished, you know,— evaporated, so to speak — that is, they were not, as it were.

He continues : "Tell me that back of Christ there is a God, who for unnumbered centuries has gone on creating men and sweeping them like dead flies — nay, living ones — into hell, is to ask me to worship a being as much worse than the conception of any mediæval devil as can be imagined, but I will not worship the devil though he should come and sit on the throne of Jehovah."

Well, who tells him of such a God? Or who asks him to worship such a being? Not the Bible! Not Christ! Not Christianity! Who then?

Ever since one brave soldier hurled his battle flag right into the midst of the phalanxes of the enemy, and then, leading on his comrades to the rescue, overthrew the armies opposed to him, quite a number of other brave fellows have tried the same experiment and come out minus a flag. And though no one will dispute the dauntless courage of the General of the Plymouth forces, and even accord to him all the qualities of a brave soldier, which I am told sometimes includes profanity in the heat of action, still there will, no doubt, be found many who will question his qualities as a commander, for we find that, having hurled his banner into the ranks of the enemy, his battalions were not equal to the emergency of rescuing it. What he may accomplish when he brings up his reserves remains a

question of the future, and in the meantime
the flag is with the enemy.

If Col. Ingersoll does not flaunt that banner from the flagstaff of Infidelity for some
time to come, I shall be greatly surprised.

Mr. Beecher and Mr. Ingersoll and the host
of other sympathetic natures whom Mr.
Beecher's words here represent, are possessed
of two errors that have been quite common to
such noble natures for more than a century.
They are these:

First. Accepting what the commentators
say of the Bible instead of what the Bible
says itself. And

Second. Permitting their imaginations instead of their judgments to take command
of their sympathies.

The first argues much for their faith in
humanity, the second for their goodness of
heart; and yet it is hardly safe to say that
either is an evidence of those qualities we
should expect to find in the leaders of a great
people.

As I have said, a complete solution of Mr.

Beecher's problem may be had by substituting the known for his unknown quantity. So far I have sought to confine the argument to the plainest truths and purest logic.

The peoples who lived and died before the Christian era went into the same eternity that we are destined to enter, and subject to the only possible difference of condition which has been wrought *by* and *through* Christ.

But leaving the relation which Christ bears to the question until it shall take its place, we will consider humanity as subject to the law of the absolute necessities: a law co-existent with every atom of matter, or pulse of mental being.

And now, under this law, let us follow the primitive races *into* eternity; let us see what disposition was made of them there, and we shall learn something, though not entirely, of the disposition that will be made of all who refuse to accept Christ.

Was there any hell awaiting them there? Was there any heaven awaiting them there? Yes, both! What kind of hell and what kind of heaven ? The same *kinds* that await you and me. But must hell exist eternally? As surely as heaven shall. Do you mean to say that a *sin* committed in this life will be *punished* throughout eternity? As surely as that a righteous act will be *rewarded* throughout eternity. Is this the law of a God of love ? Yes, for it is the law *of* being — the law necessary *to* being — the only law by which being could be made *possible !* *It is the law of the absolute necessities !*

Let us see if this can be demonstrated.

In my review of Mr. Ingersoll it was conceded that we established two propositions, which were as follows :

First. There is not an *atom* in the physical universe which is absolute, i. e., entirely independent of all other atoms.

Second. There is not a *condition* in the spiritual universe which is absolute, i. e., entirely independent of all other conditions.

Now if those two propositions are true (and, as I say, it was admitted that we proved them to be true), it matters little whether heaven or hell be places or conditions, so far as the argument to prove their eternal duration is concerned, since, in either case, neither is absolute. And so, though I cannot do violence to my sense of consistent logic by discussing either heaven or hell as a *place*, still it will be seen that what I may offer touching both, considered as conditions, will apply as forcibly to both, considered as places.

I think it will be admitted, without argument, that there are but two conditions *in* the spiritual universe — Heaven and Hell — though there may be some difference of opin ion as to degrees pertaining to each, possibly of climate, etc.; but there can be no discus- sion on the original proposition, that there are but the two conditions.

The correct definitions of the words heaven and hell — or, perhaps, I should say what I conceive to be the correct definitions — may serve us here. By heaven, then, I would im- ply the degrees of happiness, and by hell the degrees of unhappiness, that pertain to eter- nity.

Well, if there are but two conditions *in* the spiritual universe, Heaven and Hell, and if, as we have shown, there is no such possibility as an absolute condition ; or, in other words, an entirely independent condition, each must bear a relation to the other, since there is nothing else to which it can bear a relation.

What, then, follows from this?

Why, that *all* souls must go into the *same* eternity; that each soul must be subject to one of the two conditions *of* that eternity, and, if subject to one, its *possibilities* must reach to the other; or, in other words, every soul must begin the new life at just that step on the stair of development for which it has fitted itself in this life ; whether it be the soul of Homer, of Plato, of the Apostle Paul, or of Henry Ward Beecher ; whether it was fitted through the genius of poetry, of philosophy, or of Christianity, or of two of these, or of all combined. And this includes all who have lived, or ever will live, on the globe.

Well, after they begin the eternal life, then what ?

A little while ago, the question was asked: "Must hell exist eternally?" and answered, "As surely as that heaven shall."

Immediately after, another question was asked: "Do you mean to say that a sin committed in this life will be *punished* throughout eternity?" and answered: "As surely as that a righteous act will be *rewarded* throughout eternity."

Now, while I hold that we have already sustained those answers, or, rather, that they become axiomatic in the light of the principles we have established, I will proceed, notwithstanding, to make them plainer.

We will begin by asking, What is sin? and all will at once answer: Sin is the transgression of moral law. Another question: Why do men sin in this life? We shall, no doubt, agree that the answer to this is: Because they do not rightly estimate the terrible consequences of sin. It is entirely safe to assume that if men could foresee the terrible consequences of sin they would shun every form of sin, as they now shun every form of plague.

To illustrate : a man does not transgress
the law of physical being by putting his hand
in the fire, because he knows, if he does, his
hand will burn. And it would be just so in
regard to the law of moral being if he as fully
realized the certain effects that are sure to
follow certain causes.

Another thought here. It is through sin
that we sink down on the stair of moral being, and it is through righteousness that we
rise up on the stair of moral being. All this,
so far, will be conceded.

Well, in eternity we shall know the effect
of every moral law, just as well as we know
the effect here of that physical law that if we
put our hand in the fire the hand must burn.
Consequently, no one will sin, all will gradu-
ally rise higher on the stair of development
in proportion to his moral capacity.

One more thought : Nothing can be surer
than that there can be no final *landing* to the
stair of development in eternity — it must be
an eternal development — it must be infinite
in its possibilities. There is no level of

achieved pre-eminence *here*, and there can be none *there*. A fixed state or condition of happiness, however exalted, would be destructive of the very idea of happiness. Confine a man to the limits of a palace, though it be ever so grand, and it would soon become a prison ; confine a soul to the limits of a single star, though it be the greatest of the constellations, and existence would soon become unendurable.

The words heaven and hell, as usually defined, must inevitably confuse us. There can be no such possibility as a fixed *state* in eternity ; and, as we have shown, the soul in eternity can only be subject to the possibilities of a higher development.

The doctrine that all will finally be " saved," or go to heaven, is as illogical as that all will finally be " lost," or go to hell. Either is impossible.

No doubt, we should all agree were it not for the confusion of words !

Let us now select from the illustrious names of the past, Milton, Procrustes and Caligula,

three characters with whom we are all familiar.

And let us, for convenience, illustrate the
moral differences between them as so much
time. We will suppose that these began their
earth lives with equal opportunities for moral
development; and that each was, therefore,
alike responsible for his status when he
passed into eternity.

We will say that Milton's moral attainments
were such that when he passed the portals of
death and entered into eternal life, he was a
thousand years beyond Procrustes on the stair
of development, and that, for like reasons, Procrustes was a thousand years beyond Caligula.

Now, none of us believe that the future
state will be an idle, do-nothing one: no
doubt we shall all agree that it must be an
active, progressive one.

Well, these three begin in eternity with these
relative differences between them.

You will at once see the justice that puts
Milton beyond Procrustes, and Procrustes beyond such a man as Caligula. You will say

5*

it is but a mete reward — an equitable adjust-
ment — the *justice* of which each will himself
acknowledge.   You will say that anything
less than this would not be in keeping with
the eternal love and justice of God.   You will
say that anything less than this would be an
outrage upon the simplest principles of equity.
Everybody would say so; Christians, Infidels,
Pagans, the very savages of the deserts and
wildernesses, would say so; the sunbeam that
quickens the perfect before the imperfect grain
of corn would say so; the dew that kisses
the one before the other has peeped above its
earth-bed would say so; the zephyr that plays
through its brighter, stronger, nobler blades
would say so; and the husbandman who
gathers the fruit of the one into his garner,
and casts the other away, would say so; all
heaven and earth, and the things that are
under the earth, would say so.

And all these would say that it was but just
and equitable that each should occupy his
position of relative superiority throughout
eternity; since, whenever that should cease,

equity would cease and justice would cease, and, consequently, love, that rewards the good, would cease.

Surely we can all agree in this. But do you not see that what is Milton's reward becomes Procrustes' punishment? and that what is Procrustes' reward becomes Caligula's punishment, and so on down the scale of being?

It is Milton's punishment that he is a thousand years beneath what he might have been, and it is Procrustes' punishment that he is a thousand years beneath Milton, and it is Caligula's punishment that he is a thousand years beneath Procrustes; and if there is any poor wretch lower in the scale of being than Caligula he must be near the utterly deepest bottom of perdition.

And since those relative positions must be maintained throughout eternity, as each rises up on the stair of development, rewards and punishments must continue throughout eternity, and it is simply *impossible* that one can continue without the continuance of the other.

The absolute necessities demand that it must be so! For the only possible difference between Good and Bad, Pure and Impure, Wise and Unwise, Strength and Weakness, Day and Night, Happiness and Unhappiness, Heaven and Hell, and everything in God's universe, is a *comparative* difference!

But do you make heaven and hell to occupy the same space? Yes and No. Yes, since they will occupy the same eternity. No, since the pure and the impure will not be found together. And this law is in harmony with the moral law of society on our own little planet.

In regard to our first answer, "Yes," let me ask the question: Is there more than one eternity? Surely not. Well, where would you draw a line through space? How build a wall in ether?

Again: Is not God omnipresent? The Bible and your catechisms, and the scientists and everybody else says He is, and you will have to answer yes along with them. Now, do you not see that you cannot have a separate *place*

for hell? for God must be there and everywhere if He is omnipresent.

What, then, follows from this? Why, that
heaven and hell are but conditions of the
same eternity.

Now, in regard to our second answer, " No,"
let me ask the question : What is more repellent to a good and pure man or woman than
the society of the corrupt and wicked? or
what is more repellent to a corrupt and
wicked man or woman than the society of
the good and pure? Here, in Chicago, you
have your churches and a society of pure
men and women; you have also your slums
of vice and their pitiable inmates,— do these
divisions of society mix together?

In eternity, every soul that is dwarfed or
maimed by sin or impurity will be recognized
as readily as a dwarfed or maimed *body* is recognized on earth, and they will shrink from
the eye of the pure, and call upon the mountains to bury them from the eye of God.

But will the sorrows of hell be as terrible as
the Bible depicts them? This is a horrible

thought, and yet one that every man can answer for himself.

The scientists and philosophers will tell you that the suffering of the body is slight when compared to the suffering of the mind. — A strong willed soldier, once, amputated his own limb, and then seared the bleeding, sensitive wound with a red hot gun barrel, and so stopped the effusion of blood and recovered. Years after, he struck down his brother, in anger, and the brother died — *and the soldier died of remorse!* He could endure the amputation of his own limb, and endure the torture of the seething iron, burning into his quivering flesh, but he could not endure the *remorse* that followed his sin.

Show me the Bible's picture of hell, and I will show you a soul haunted by itself through eternity with remorse proportioned to its crimes. What is lost through sin, though it be but a loss of time, can never be recovered.

When Mr. Beecher talks about " the inroad of that vast amount of mud swept into

heaven as destructive of its purity," and when
he talks about "sweeping them like dead flies
— nay living ones — into hell," he indulges
in a metaphor that out-Ingersolls Ingersoll,
nay out-Beechers Beecher. It is without
parallel even in the long record of Plymouth's
erratic pastor, or in the annals of our primitive western eloquence, or yet in the pristine
purity of plantation pulpit philology.

It becomes necessary to quote from Mr.
Beecher, again, for he again represents a
large element of society in the position he
assumes. But it is hard to believe that a
man who has stood at the head and front
of American moral philosophers so long,
could say what he does, even with the record
before us. He says :

"Now, that the race should be put in this
world at so low a point would not be strange,
any more than it is strange that a man cuts a
little twig off from a rose-bush, and puts it
in a thumb-pot one inch across, and sets it on
a table in a propagating house, with bottom
heat, if the moral problem were the same as

the physical one — where there is the instrumentality for germinating the twig, where there is a gardener to care for it, to shift it, to develop it, to give it room and opportunity for growth and maturity.

" But that has not been the history of the human race. Mankind are thrown abroad on this continent in myriads, and we know that not only their happiness but their morality largely depends on their knowledge of how to use their bodies, and how to control the natural laws that surround them ; but on these subjects not a word nor a syllable is told them."

If the old Testament tells us anything, it tells us that from the time man was cut from the original bush and placed in the thumb-pot of Eden, to the dawn of the Christian era, the great Gardener of the universe took the tenderest care of him, shifted him, straightened him, and gave him every opportunity for growth and development. And you *know* this is so, and I know this is so, and every reader of that Old Testament knows it is so.

And we know, besides, that, perhaps, there never was a plant that gave a gardener so much trouble. And we are inclined to *think* that we have a forcible illustration of what that original plant was in the erratic pastor of Plymouth Church.

Mr. Beecher continues:

" The sweep of the populations that have swarmed on the globe is simply inconceivable. . . . Not all the waves of the ocean that have beaten on its shores during all the centuries of time contained drops enough. . . . Not all the sands of the sea-shore, all the stars of heaven and .all the figures of arithmetic."—Well, we haven't time to compute it, you know,—" and during three fourths of its history the race was without an altar, or a church, or an authorized priest, a revelation, or anything but the light of nature."

Now, when Mr. Beecher antedates so, in order to sustain his mathematics, what can he *know* about "three-fourths" of those prehistoric times ? or one-fourth, or, indeed, any part except what the Old Testament speaks

6

of? He is dealing here very vigorously in assertions. There is a bound even to poetic pastures, beyond which are the fields called pure fiction.

> "Ever to that truth,
> Which but the semblance of a falsehood wears,
> A man, if possible, should bar his lip."
>
> *Dante's Inferno, Canto XVI.*

Well, how does Mr. Beecher reconcile the terrible state of things he depicts here?

Why, after sleepless nights and throes of agony, amidst grave doubts and graver responsibilities, and visions of reformers pelted and beaten, and visions of the persecutions of advanced thinkers,—after all this and much more of like character, descriptive of the labor of the mountain, behold the twin thoughts that are brought forth: "God's ways are not our ways," and, "What is time with us is not time with God,"—two old theological saws that have ruined work wherever they have been used; two answers that have made more infidels than Mr. Beecher has hairs in his venerable head. And yet if you will boil down Mr. Beecher's answers, and let the

rhetorical steam evaporate, this is all you
will have left. And I quote these answers
not in irreverence to their great author, but
because they are fair samples of many of
the answers that have been given on one
side of this question, and are only matched,
I think, by the entire negation of the infidels
on the other side.

If you please, we will now take up the
theory of creation, the law of being, and discuss it from the scientific standpoint. I desire, as the first step, to lay down what I
conceive to be three incontrovertible propositions ; three propositions that become axiomatic when viewed in the light of pure
philosophy and reason. They are as follows :

First. There is but *one*, and there could by
no possibility be more than *one*, universe.

Second. There is but *one*, and there could by
no possibility be more than one, set of
laws for that one universe.

Third. Every *law* of that *one* universe must
be in perfect harmony with every *other*
law of that *one* universe.

Here, then, we have struck three bed-rock truths of both science and philosophy. Infidels, Christians, everybody,— Huxley, Tyndall, Baine, Ingersoll, Beecher, Prof. Swing, the Apostle Paul, everybody,— will indorse these. So far we are all agreed. And now let us keep our minds free from all entangling alliances, and all special theories, for a little while. And please do not anticipte what is coming!

I shall not lead you into any of the old paths. I am wedded to no sect, no school of metaphysics or theology, and I shall only ask that *you* shall not be for the little while that remains to us. I am merely an earnest, and, I trust, honest seeker for truth, and I propose to follow *the straight path of pure logic* wherever it shall lead me, beginning with these three *facts* we have before us — these three incontrovertible truths. And if we do this it is impossible that we should go wrong. But we must not swerve from the straight line,— no, not the breadth of ahair. Though old familiar forms and faces, that have been the companions of other days, shall beckon us from either side, aye, though they may have been our school-fellows, or may have knelt with us at the altar through three-score years and ten, yet must we not swerve from the straight path of logic the millionth part of a point, or every step will but lead us farther away.

The only reason that all men do not reach the same conclusion is that they train their logic to subserve some pet idea, instead of letting it take its own pure logical path. We can all agree upon the foundation *facts* as a starting point ; but we are apt to fly the track when we discover that it doesn't lead to " our meetin'-house."

Well, if there is but *one* universe, and if there could by no possibility *be* more than one universe, as claimed in our first proposition, and if every law of that one universe must be in harmony with every *other* law of that one universe as claimed in our two subsequent propositions, it follows that if we find *one single law* that is absolutely necessary *to* that one universe we have found a law with which all other laws *must* work in harmony.

We are still agreed.

Now I affirm that the law of development is one of those laws. Don't anticipate!

Let us see if we can find that law in existence, and then let us see if it is one of the primary laws, or fundamental laws; or, in other words, one of the laws absolutely necessary *to* existence. If we find that it is, we will have found a law with which all other laws *must* work in harmony.

We will seek, first, in the world of matter. We will take a grain of corn.

In the order of its being, corn must proceed from the germ of life that is in the grain; must receive nutrition from the earth, and warmth from the sun's rays, before it can burst its shell; these are the first operations that link it to the earth, and link it to solar heat. Then it leaps up from the earth, and is embraced by the arms of the light, and kissed by the zephyrs of morning, to be received, amid the perfume of grasses and the song of

flowers, upon the loving breast of the glorious day. Thus is it taken into fellowship,
and thus does it become a part of the world ;
thus is it allied to the physical universe, and
thus is it put in possession of its identity.
This is the law of its being, which, we shall
find, is in harmony with the laws of all physical being.

But, at this point, the question arises, *Why*
this arbitrary law, this *gradual* process? *Why*
could it not have been different, so that other
laws should be different in conformity to it?
This would, no doubt, be Mr. Ingersoll's
inquiry, were he here. *Why?* Because anything else were *impossible!* This is another
one of the *absolute necessities.* I think we
can demonstrate this.

Suppose I wish to bring my hands together
— they are now some distance apart — I bring
them together ; it was a gradual movement,
requiring a full second of time. Suppose I
bring them together with the greatest possible
speed ; it was a less gradual movement than
before, but gradual, nevertheless.

The electric flash of the lightning is very quick; it seems to cleave the air in an instant; but it is a gradual movement. The first strata of air are pierced before the second, and the second before the third, and the first stratum, or wave of the first strata, of air is divided before the second wave of the first strata is divided.

Now, in order that the grand harmony of the universe should be maintained, it was necessary that there should be a relationship, or fellowship, of all things, animate and inanimate. And so if we take up the orders of the lower animals, we find them closely allied to the little grain of corn. We find similar and harmonious laws applying to them that apply to vegetable life. We find them proceeding from a *germ*, and by a *gradual movement* undergoing the process of development. And we find them linked to the physical universe, not only by the *laws* by which they have reached the full stature of maturity, but by the very composition of their nerves and fibers and tissues. All this was necessary if

the grand harmony of the universe be maintained.

Let us follow the logical path a little farther.

Now, if there is but *one*, and if there could
by no possibility *be* more than one, universe,
and if there can be but *one* set of laws for the
one universe, and if those laws must work in
perfect harmony, it follows that the only *possibility* of *existence* must be *in* the one universe, since there is no other ; and every existence *in* the one universe must be subject
to the *one* set of *laws* in the one universe,
and every law in the *one* universe must be
in perfect harmony with every other law in
the one universe.

Well, if the only *possibility* of existence is in
the *one* universe, it follows that the existence
of *man* must be in the *one* universe ; and since
there can be but *one* set of laws in the *one*
universe, it follows that man must be subject
to that one set of laws ; and since every law
in the one universe *must* work in perfect harmony with every *other* law in the *one* universe,

it follows that the law of man's physical being must be in harmony with all other laws of physical being. *And so we find man,* as in the case of the vegetables, and the different orders of animals, linked to the physical universe, not only by the *laws* by which he has reached the full stature of maturity, but by the very composition of his body. All this was necessary to preserve the sublime harmony of the universe.

We come now to speak of man's immortal part, his spiritual nature ; for this, too, must be a part of the grand harmony of all things.

What is the scientific bed-rock ? Why, that there are but two things in the universe — *matter* and *mind.* What does science tell us that man is composed of ? Matter and mind. What does the Bible tell us that man is composed of ? " Dust of the earth," or matter, and " breath of life," or mind. Man, then, becomes the great connecting link between matter and God. Of all things, man alone is composed of the two materials — matter and mind ; so if there were such a condition as a double neces·

sity, we should say that it becomes doubly necessary that man should be in perfect har mony with the universe, should we not, since he occupies the relation he does to both elements of the universe?

Let us see if we cannot demonstrate that man not only *is*, but that the law of spiritual existence demands, nay, makes it the condition *of*, the absolute necessity *to* his being, that he be in perfect harmony with this law of development.

Now, if we show that there are necessities to thought, it follows that we have shown necessities to mind.

So, if we find that the law absolutely necessary *to* thought is the same law which we found necessary to matter, i. e., the law of development, of gradual movement, we shall have found a law as necessary to mind and soul.

(We cannot pause here to discuss the difference between mind and soul, but must reserve that for another time. In a word, I hold that mind is the connecting link between the body

and the soul, and that *thought* is that extraneous, indefinable something which is communicated by the soul, through the mind, to
the body.)

Well, you will admit that, though a thought
is very quick in its movement (and hence we
sometimes say, as quick as thought),— that a
thought may not pass through the mind in
an instant.   I think we can realize this when
we recall our personal experience, wherein it
has required quite a little while to get some
thoughts through our minds.   Possibly the
present may be one of those instances.   Let
us try to make it plainer : a thought must
first enter the brain, and the brain becomes the
medium through which it is communicated
to the body, and then the body acts in
obedience to the thought.

Or, to recall the figure we took from the
material world, a flash of lightning is very
quick in its action, but it must cleave the air,
strata by strata ; the stratum or wave that
is nearest it must always be pierced first,
before it can reach the second wave, and it is

just so with a thought; it must enter the
first wave of mind, if you will permit the
figure, before it can enter the second wave
of mind, and the second before it can enter
the third, and so on till it has passed *through*
the mind.

This illustration serves us in understanding that the law is universal, and applies to
small thoughts as well as great; and that
the development of a thought is the process
of a movement to an idea, or that thought
is a process *of* development, and consequently subject to the *law* of development.
Therefore the law of development is absolutely necessary *to* thought, and if to thought,
to mind and soul.

What, then, is the deduction?— it is *very*
plain, and it is very *sure*,—why, this :

The condition *of* man's being, the absolute
necessity *to* man's being, demands that he be
in perfect harmony with the universe — the
laws and *conditions* of the universe. And
since there is and could *be* but one universe,
and there is and could *be* but one set of laws,

therefore the laws and conditions to which the human race is subject are the *only* laws and conditions, physical and spiritual, by which existence in the absolute could be made *possible*.

From this very simple arrangement of very simple truths it follows that man was not placed on this earth by the caprice of a Creator, but in harmony with immutable law. Immutable, because it were *impossible* that it should be different from just what it is. And this is just as sure as that there is and could by no possibility *be* but one universe; and that there is and could by no possibility *be* but *one set of laws* for that *one* universe; and that there is and could by no possibility *be* but one God *of* that one universe!

Philosophies here center! Upon this mountain top that overlooks the world, this everlasting rock on which is set the azimuth stair of God, lo, we may challenge every school of science and of thought, for the conception of a law of being other than this! It is absolutely inconceivable!

When Mr. Beecher and Mr. Ingersoll fret
and scold about the slow and plodding
progress of humanity, they are but fretful
children, whining of the winter's cold, or
scolding the bright sunbeams in the sum-
mer's noon.

The slow and plodding progress of humanity is but the gradual though sure development of man. And when Mr. Beecher and
Mr. Ingersoll and Mr. Thomas Paine, and
the little army of little philosophical guer-
rillas that train under them, fret and scold
because He, whom they call an "omnipotent
God of love," did not *force* knowledge and
enlightenment upon the human race, instead
of leaving it to the freedom of an untrammeled *will* and its own development, they are
not less children or less deserving of our pity.

It was upon the foundation of *free, untrammeled will* that the superstructure of the
mind was built. It was through the principle of *free untrammeled will* that Attain-
ment reached down from her sublime heights
and clasped the hand of Endeavor. It is

by the talismanic power of *free, untrammeled will* that man leaps from earth to heaven, knocks at its door and is admitted to the court of angels.

A story is told of a North American Indian chief, who stood watching an engine and its train of cars as it came rushing into a station of the Pacific railroad. An expression of stoic dignity set every line of his bronzed features. He walked up to the engine and regarded it closely. It did not move now. The engineer had leaped off the opposite side unobserved by the savage, and so no one was about it. He watched it to see if it would give any signs of life, but it did not move. Presently the engineer sprang up to his place; he pulled a bar, and it screamed; he pulled another bar, and it breathed heavily; he pulled another bar, it trembled, it moved; and as *it* rushed away the *Indian* turned, and, grunting his contempt, strode proudly over the plain.

A man is a wonderful piece of machinery, but it is the freedom of his *will* that makes him a demigod. Man is a wonderful piece of

machinery, but take away from him the freedom of his *will* and he would be no more
than that engine that was the contempt of a
savage.

This brings us to the advent of Christ. It
will not be expected that we can, at this time,
enter into a lengthy discussion of the relation
of Christ to humanity, or of His *peculiar* relation to those who accept, believe and obey
Him. And yet I hold that even these may
be scientifically demonstrated by axiomatic
truths and their purest logical deductions.

We can only, at present, pass through so
much as becomes, at this point, necessary to
the immediate question before us.

It would not do to draw a comparison between nations in discussing a subject so cos-
mical in its character as the one before us, or
it were easy to show that Christianity and
Enlightenment go hand in hand. Should I
compare the nations of earth, I should speak
of my own America. I should hail her as the
land beyond all others! I should crown her
Queen of Nations!

6*

"My country ! Oh, of thee,
    Sweet land of Liberty.
    Of thee I'd sing;
    Till from thy rocks and rills,
    Thy woods and templed hills,
    Wherever rapture thrills,
        Thy name should ring."

But, now, our song must not be confined to a national soprano, it must be attuned to the sublime chorus that is joined wherever man is free, wherever woman is pure, wherever knowledge is triumphant, wherever virtue is rewarded, wherever the chimes of sabbath bells are heard, and the children are glad on Christmas morn.

The effect of the Christian system, as seen in the enlightenment of the human race, is evident to all; Christianity needs no en-comium at my hands. I will only drop in one item here, and one which, I think, may be clearly demonstrated. It is this:

As *advanced thought* is the food necessary to the higher development of the mind, so is *Christianity* the food necessary to the highest development of the soul; and as the mind must be developed to a certain point before it can receive advanced thought, so must the soul be developed to a certain point before it can receive Christianity. From this it will be seen that Christianity, considered from a scientific standpoint, is a system of psychological development. But considered from a theological standpoint, there is a question of *atonement*, which we must leave for another time.

It is sometimes asked: Why was not Christ sent into the world at an earlier period? Christ was sent into the world just as soon as the human race was ready to receive Him. But you will say there were times prior to His coming when the world was farther advanced in the arts and sciences than at the time He did come. Very true; but not on the stair of *moral* being. Though *we* may not be able to mark the distinction between the intellectual and the moral, God is, and He did it.

The enlightened of the human race had Moses just as soon as they were ready to receive him, and they had the prophets just as

soon as they were ready to receive them ; and
then came John the Baptist, and then Christ,
in fulfillment of the great law of being. Well,
what is that law of being? Why, this : that
just as fast as humanity is capable of development, just that fast are the means of development given. This is a law as universal as
the love of God ; it is a law that permeates
every atom of matter and every condition of
mind. As fast as the blade of grass requires
nutrition of the earth it is supplied through
its roots, and as oft as it thirsts it may drink
of the dew, and as oft as it calls for the sunbeam, as oft does it feel the sunbeam's kiss.

When a babe is born into the world it requires the daintiest thoughts, and these are
supplied through its delicate mind. When
the babe is grown to a child, it is given the
birds and the flowers. When the child is a
maiden, or youth,· it has music, and twilight,
and stars, and love and sighs ; and when
the full stature of manhood and womanhood
comes, we have thought —we have thought —
and communion with God ! And these are

inexhaustible! And these shall endure forever!

And this leads us to another point — the
Sacrifice of Christ. Why was it necessary
that *He* should be sacrificed? *He*, the Pure,
the Immaculate One?

The answer is simple and plain — *In obedience to law!* the law of the eternal necessities! — the law that sits on the throne of
Jehovah, touches the harp of the universe, and
attunes the sweet song of the stars!

Why, there is *nothing* that is not subject to
the law of sacrifice! The flower that blooms
in your garden, exhaling its rare perfumes,
was only produced through sacrifice of earth,
and air, and sunlight, and dew. The pebble
that lies in the brooklet, the granite that
stands by the sea-shore, were only produced
through sacrifice, and the labor of years and
years! And man is produced through sacrifice, and travail, and groans, and is only sustained through sacrifice of millions and millions of atoms, of millions and millions of
lives!

And when that great, grand work was at
hand — the higher development and redemp-
tion of man — no less a sacrifice was demanded than Christ, the Son of God.

This brings us to the closing thought —
Miracles.

We have reached the dangerous pass in
our logical path ; but let us not falter ! Our
path is along a narrow ledge, but it is straight
ahead ; let us not falter now ! It is very narrow, but it is firm, it is sure, it is God's own
granite, its base is deep in the earth ! It is
narrow, but it is plain, it stands out clean cut
through the ether ; let us not falter ! We
have reached its dizziest height ; as you are
a man, do not falter ! as you are a man, press
on !

Is not every miracle a violation of law ?
No ! There never was a miracle in violation
of law ! God never broke a single law of the
universe ! What, then *is* miracle ? The exercise of *God's reserve power*, in obedience
to law.

What do you mean ? Why, this : Professor

Morse knew the law of electrical currents, and
the laws of atmosphere, and of light, and of
heat, and of metals; and he had the power to
use these as other people did. But back of
this he had a *reserve power*. What was that?
Why, to manipulate those different laws, and
without disturbing their harmony, so as to
produce the telegraph; and ignorant men
called *that* a miracle.

Well, just so God holds a *reserve power*.
This is a quality of His omniscience that is
equal to any emergency. The absolute necessity *to* omniscience is that it *be* equal to *all*
emergencies. God has the power to use all
the laws of the universe just as we use them,
but back of this He has a *reserve power* by
which he can manipulate these, and without
disturbing their harmony, so as to produce
miracles. Men are performing miracles every
day to the extent of that *power* that their
limited wisdom contains and holds in *reserve*
for emergencies. But as God's wisdom is unlimited, His *reserve power* is equal to all emergencies.

Science is fast bringing these things to the light of human intelligence.

What scientists perform, now, every day, were declared impossible a few years ago; and what we deem impossible, now, will, no doubt, be simple and plain in a few years hence. For just as fast as the mind calls for food, just that fast is the mind supplied. And as oft as the Soul shall call to its God, as oft shall its God answer: Here am I.

Now, the miracles of the Apostles were beyond the miracles of Franklin, and Morse, and Fulton. Why? Because they were not performed by the Apostles, but by God. Theirs was a delegated power,—they wrought through pure faith, not knowledge. Christ told them, before He went away, that when one of these difficult, scientific problems was presented, to send it up to Him, and He would solve it. And they followed His instructions, and He *did* solve every problem that they sent up to the court of heaven. He did not show the figures or the demonstration of *how* they were done, for they could not have comprehended them, but He sent the correct "answer." every time. And He is solving problems for us every day. We get into trouble and we pray to Him, and He helps us out of it. We don't know *how* it is done, but when the *load* is lifted from our hearts we know that it *is* done. And every time this is done, a miracle is performed. It may be only a very small miracle, sometimes,— small when compared to the raising of Lazarus from the tomb,— but it is a miracle nevertheless. And when we come to put on immortality He will solve *that* problem, and in obedience to law.

I said, a few moments ago :

"Science is fast bringing these things to the light of human intelligence." Science is doing it — or God is doing it— or both ; may be, after all, they are but one, if we only knew what we were talking about. Science is bringing great truths to light — though some of the scientists are submitting to the results of their own experiments with very ill grace.

Why, a few years ago the Infidels said that

7

the idea of Christ's miraculous conception was so opposed to all reason and law, that it, in itself, overthrew the entire Christian philosophy.

Well, Huxley and Bain, and a score of other scientists and specialists, started out to settle the whole question with the microscope.

This was their last ditch, and they proposed to rout us here. What is the result? If you will turn to the recent ninth edition of the " Encyclopedia Britannica," you will find, in the article on Biology, by Professor Huxley, page 687, these words:

" Generation by fission and gemmation are not confined to the simplest forms of life. Both modes are common, not only among plants, but among animals of considerable complexity."

Again:

" Through almost the whole series of living beings we find agamo-genesis, or not-sexual generation."

And Bain and the score of others who

started out to *crush* Christianity, indorse what Mr. Huxley says here.

Well, when they found this law existing throughout the vegetable and throughout the animal kingdoms, *except in the case of man*, then what did they say?

Why, that what was called the miraculous conception of Christ could only have been a freak of nature — an accident!

Oh, it is a pitiable sight when great men are reduced to such straits as this! It is a sad commentary on the doctrine of universal honesty. "It just *happened* so." Things don't *happen* so in this universe of law. The genus of Chance does not preside over this little planet — for, if it did, there would be no end to the *happenings*. If it did, Mr. Ingersoll might have been Pope Leo XIII, and Mr. Beecher might have been less given to sensations.

Now, what *is* the deduction from this great truth that the microscope reveals to us,— or that God reveals to us through the microscope,— that the law of agamo-genesis, or not-

sexual generation *exists?* Why, if the law
exists, then it must be in harmony with all
other laws of the universe, as we found a
while ago ; and if it applies to the vegetables
and the higher orders of animals, as the
scientists have demonstrated, it is in *God's
reserve power* that it may be applied to *man*
without the infraction of any law of the universe. And, therefore, God only used His
reserve power when He *did* apply it in the
miraculous conception of Christ.

But you will say : In the vegetables, and
animals below man, this law of not-sexual
generation invariably produces the same effects. Very true,— there can be nothing
truer than that like causes produce like effects. That which became the *cause* in the
orders below man was simply the result of
the exercise of the ordinary power of the law
as applied to their several species, invariably
producing the same effects : that which became the *cause* in the conception of Christ
was the result of the exercise of the reserve
power of God ; and, to conclude logically,

we must hold that a like effect could only proceed from a like cause, and that, therefore, there has been but ône Christ.

Now, does this idea of the reserve power of God, as we have applied it, detract from the omnipotence of Deity? Not at all. On the contrary, to my mind, it exalts the thought of Omnipotence by linking it to Omniscience. To my mind, it introduces us to a higher, nobler conception of God. Why? Upon the old theory, the laws of the universe (of which it is held that God was the author and maker) were such that it became necessary, in order to meet emergencies, that God should break them or make new ones. In other words, these laws which God made were so imperfect that the Deity was constantly putting them through a course of repairs. Upon the theory we have endeavored to present in this paper, the laws of the universe are perfect and equal to all emergencies. In our ignorance we may understand them only to the extent of finite intelligence: in God's wisdom He under-

stands them to the extent of infinite intelligence — Omniscience.

I am so constituted that I could not worship a God who ruled through imperfect laws.
If His laws were imperfect I should conclude
that He must be an imperfect God. The God
I worship is a *perfect* God. He is Omniscient, Omnipotent and Omnipresent. He is
a *perfect* God, and He rules through *perfect*
laws.

Now, we must accept one of the two conclusions : Miracles are either wrought in obedience to law or by the infraction of law.
No one can take exception to this proposition. Well, then, I accept the former upon
the theory of Reserve Power. Who accepts
the latter must be met by this incontrovertible, scientific fact : *The infraction of the least
possible law of the universe would bring confusion and universal chaos;* since there is
but *one* universe, but *one* set of laws for that
one universe, and every law *in* that one universe must work in perfect harmony with
every *other* law in that one universe; and,

therefore, every law is dependent upon every
other law for the continuation of its own existence.

I think it will be conceded that we have
proven the *possibility* of what are called *miracles.* The Infidels must now meet the *evidence*
of the records, which they never have done.
They have simply set the whole question of
miracles aside by declaring that they were *impossible*, as an infraction of law was an impos-
sibility. But we have found that miracles may
be wrought without the infraction of law, and,
as I say, now they must meet the *evidence*.

The question has often been asked, why
God did not send Christ direct from heaven,
in the full stature of physical and intellectual
development; or, in other words, what was
the necessity of Christ's being born of a
woman, and that He should rest on the breast
of a mother, and listen to her gentle lullaby,
and dally with the sunbeams, as a child, and
drink in the sweet significance of the flowers;
and that he should revel with youth in the
bird songs and the hymns of the Zephyrs at

eventide ; that He should rise step by step to manhood, as every man must on this earth ; and that He should die, and be buried, and rise again ;—was it that He should know our condition here? Yes, but more than this,— that He should know it as we know it! Yes, for He knew it as God before : but more than this,— that he should *learn* it as *we* learn it, *in obedience to law !* Christ was conceived through *God's reserve power* that there should be no infraction of law. He was born of woman that there should be no infraction of law. He passed through all the stages of development that there should be no infraction of law. He died, was buried, and was resurrected that there should be no infraction of law. God never did break a law and He never will break a law! Every law of the universe is in harmony with the very law of God's own being, and to break a law would be to break Himself. And this is just as sure as that there is but one universe, and that there is but one God *of* that *one* universe.

"The universe is governed by *law!*" says Humboldt, and Ingersoll takes up the refrain and cries, "the universe is governed by *law!*" "A *second* Daniel come to judgment! I thank thee, Jew, for teaching me that word! Now, Infidel, I have thee on the hip!"

Christianity is a science, and the most accurate of all the sciences. It is the foundation of the purest philosophy. It is the science of the soul. It is the science by which God leads us up to Himself. And its laws are as sure as the foundations of the universe.

And as sure as good deeds will be rewarded, just that sure must evil deeds be punished; for this is the law *of* existence; the law necessary *to* existence; the law by which existence is made *possible;* the only law by which existence *could* be made possible;— it is the law of the Absolute Necessities.

And the Bible is the one book that contains that part of that law which pertains to the soul; the one indestructible, immutable temple that was built by God to contain the Sacred Treasures.

Let the storms of Infidelity rage, though they be ever so loud! Let thoughtless youth and decaying old age sport as oft as they may with the perilous winds! The storm shall roll on and be lost in the night, but the temple shall stand as before!

Be ye not deceived, for our Lord is not mocked!

The storm shall roll on and be lost in the night, and the night it shall pass, and then cometh the morn and the light! and then we shall *see*, and shall *know*, and our voices shall sing a sweet song, attuned to the song of the stars! We shall join the grand chorus of worlds!

A chorus that began with the faint muffled purl of nebulæ — was touched to measure by His voice who said, "Let there be light!" then joined by the resonant waves of the deep; and when the waters were together drawn, by cascade and rill, brook, river and sea!

A chorus that caught up the million-voiced rhythm, the first sweet song of nature, and the first wild rhapsody of universal life!

A chorus whose reverberations melt into oneness the harmonious cycles of the past, and in whose echoes every moment finds a perfect register!

A chorus that *now* joins the melodious voices of every sylvan bower and glen! of every bright, sun-kissed floral vale! of the vast fields, rich with their golden grain! of vaster plains run wild in liberty! aye, of the very deserts whose bright sands reflect the marvelous music of the sunbeams!

A chorus that unites both hemispheres, whose mountains echo, and whose rivers bear, the illimitable, grand refrain!

A chorus that leaps into the clouds! grasps the thunder! sweeps through the corridors of the universe! rises into the translucent ether! mounts the azimuth stair of the Infinite, and rests at last at the very throne of the Eternal God!

ROBERT'S RULES OF ORDER, For Deliberative Assemblies.—

By Major H. M. Robert, Corps of Engineers, U. S. A.   Pocket size, cloth, 75 cents.

This book is far superior to any other parliamentary manual in the English language.   It gives in the simplest form possible all the various rules or points of law or order that can arise in the deliberations of any lodge, grange, debating club, literary society, convention, or other organized body, and every rule is complete in itself, and as easily found as a word in a dictionary.   Its crowning excellence is a "Table of Rules relating to Motions," on two opposite pages which contains the answers to more than two hundred questions on parliamentary law, which will be of the greatest value to every member of an assembly.

"It should be studied by all who wish to become familiar with the correct usages of public meetings."—*E. O. Haven, D. D., Chancellor of Syracuse University.*

"It seems much better adapted to the use of societies and assemblies than either Jefferson's Manual or Cushing's."—*J. M. Gregory, LL. D., late President of the Illinois Industrial University.*

"I shall be very glad to see your Manual brought into general use, as I am sure it must be, when its great merit and utility become generally known.—*Hon. 'I M. Cooley, LL. D , author of ' Cooley's Blackstone,' " etc.*

"After carefully examining it and comparing it with several other books having the same object in view, I am free to say that it is, by far, the best of all. The 'Table of Rules' is worth the cost of the work."—*Thomas Bowman, D. D., Bishop of Baltimore M. E. Conference.*

"This capital little manual will be found exceedingly useful by all who are concerned in the organization or management of societies of various kinds.   .   .   . If we mistake not, the book will displace all its predecessors, as an authority on parliamentary usages."—*New York World.*

"I admire the plan of your work, and the simplicity and fidelity with which you have executed it.   It is one of the best compendiums of Parliamentary Law that I have seen, and exceedingly valuable, not only for the matter usually embraced in such a book, but for its tables and incidental matter, which serve greatly to adapt it to common use."—*Dr. D. C. Eddy, Speaker of the Massachusetts House of Representatives.*

MISHAPS OF MR. EZEKIEL PELTER.—Illustrated.

12mo, cloth...$1.50.

"So ludicrous are the vicissitudes of the much-abused Ezekiel, and so much of human nature and every-day life intermingle, that it will be read with a hearty zest for its *morals*, while the humor is irresistible.   If you want to laugh at something new, a regular side-splitter, get this book."—*The Evangelist, St. Louis.*

"We have read Ezekiel. We have laughed and cried over its pages. It grows in interest to the last sentence.   The story is well told, and the moral so good, that we decidedly like and commend it."—*Pacific Baptist, San Francisco.*

WORDS; THEIR USE AND ABUSE, By Prof. Wm. Mathews,

Author of "Getting on in the World," "The Great Conversers," Etc.,.........$2 00.

"A book of rare interest."—*Brooklyn Eagle.*

"Every page sparkles with literary gems."—*The Interior.*

"An interesting, well-written and instructive volume."—*Independent, N. Y.*

"Every literary man and woman should read it."—*Sunday Times, N. Y.*

"A valuable companion for writers, talkers and people generally."—*Boston Journal.*

"Although written for popular reading, they are scholarly and instructive, and in a very high degree entertaining. No one can turn to a single page of the book without finding something worth reading and worth remembering. It is a book both for libraries and general reading, as scholars will not disdain its many valuable illustraions, while the rising writer will find in it a perfect wealth of rules and suggestions to help him form a good style of expression."—*Publishers' Weekly, New York.*

"To this large class, (the great body of our people in every rank, occupation and profession) it will prove a most entertaining recreation and useful study. Young men in higher schools, academies and colleges will also find it a useful and helpful guide, which will not only save them from committing vulgar solecisms and awkward verbal improprieties, but from contracting vicious habits that will stick to them, if once suffered to be formed, like the shirt of Nessus."—*Christian Intelligencer, New York.*

"The final chapter on 'Common Improprieties of Speech' should be printed in tract form. . . . We should like to put a copy of this book into the hands of *every man and woman* who is using or intends to use, our good old Anglo-Saxon with voice or pen for any public service. It is a text book, full of information, and contains hints, rules, criticisms and illustrations. which authenticate their own value."—*Christian at Work, New York*

TWO YEARS IN CALIFORNIA, By Mary Cone. With 15 fine

engravings, a map of California, and a plan of the Yosemite Valley. Cloth.....$1.75

"One of the most reliable and authentic works on California yet issued."—*Sunday Times, New York.*

"One of the best descriptions of the Golden State that has met our eye, . . unbiassed, impartial, and intelligent."—*Christian at Work, New York.*

"This is a book of absorbing interest. . . No description can do justice to it. Every page deserves to be read and studied."—*Albany Journal.*

"It would be difficult to compress within the same limits more really valuable information on the subject treated than is here given."—*Morning Star, Boston.*

"Will be of much value to every one who contemplates either visiting or emigrating to California."—*New York Evening Mail.*

PUBLISHED BY S. C. GRIGGS & CO., CHICAGO.

PRE-HISTORIC RACES OF THE UNITED STATES.

By J. W. FOSTER, LL.D., Author of " The Physical Geography of the Mississippi Valley," etc. 415 pages, crown 8vo, with a large number of illustrations.

Price, cloth _____ $3 00
Half calf binding, gilt top _____ 5 00
Full calf, gilt edges _____ 6 50

" One of the best and clearest accounts we have seen of those grand monuments of a forgotten race."—*London Saturday Review.*

" The reader will find it more fascinating than his last favorite novel."—*Eclectic Magazine, N. Y.*

" The book is literally crowded with astonishing and valuable facts."—*Boston Post.*

" It is an elegant volume and a valuable contribution to the subject. * * * Contains just the kind of information in clear, compressed and intelligible form, which is adapted to the mass of readers."—*Appleton's Popular Science Monthly.*

" The book is typographically perfect, and with its admirable illustrations and convenient index is really elegant and a sort of luxury to possess and read. * * Dr. Foster's style reminds us of Tyndall and Proctor, at their best. * * He goes over the ground, inch by inch, and accumulates information of surprising interest and importance, bearing on this subject, which he gives in his crowded but most instructive and entertaining chapters in a thoroughly scientific but equally popular way. We have marked whole pages of his book for quotation, and finally from sheer necessity have been compelled to put the whole volume in quotation marks, as one of the few books that are indispensable to the student, and scarcely less important for the intelligent reader to have at hand for reference."—*Golden Age, New York.*

A MANUAL OF GESTURE.— With over 100 Figures,

embracing a complete system of Notation, with the Principles of Interpretation and Selections for Practice. By Prof. A. M. BACON.

Price _____ $1 75

" Prof. Bacon has given us a work that, in thoroughness and practical value, deserves to rank among the most remarkable books of the season. There has in fact, been no work on the subject yet offered to the public which approaches it for exhaustiveness and completeness of detail. * * It is of the utmost value, not merely to students, but to lawyers, clergymen, teachers, and public speakers, and its importance as an assistant in the formation of a correct and appropriate style of action can hardly be over-estimated."—*The Philadelphia Inquirer.*

" Prof. Bacon's Manual seems expressly arranged for the help of those who study alone and have undertaken self-instruction in the art of persuasive delivery. The work in the hands of our ministry, well studied, would have the effect of emphasizing the living words of the Gospel all over the land, and making them two-edged with meaning."—*The Chicago Pulpit.*